Bad for My Thug

Part Three

By
Miss Jenesequa

BAD FOR MY THUG 3: THE FINALE

© 2016
Published by Royalty Publishing House
www.royaltypublishinghouse.com
All rights reserved
www.missjenesequa.com

Any unauthorized reprint or use of this material is prohibited. No part of this book may be reproduced or transmitted in any form or by any means, electronic, or mechanical, including photocopying, recording, or by any information storage without express permission by the publisher.

This is a work of fiction. Names, characters, businesses, places, events and incidents are either the products of the author's imagination or used in a fictitious manner. Any resemblance to actual persons, living or dead, or actual events is purely coincidental.

Contains explicit language & adult themes suitable for ages 16+

MISS JENESEQUA

Remember….

You haven't read 'til you've read #Royalty

Check us out at
www.royaltypublishinghouse.com
Royalty drops #dopebooks

BAD FOR MY THUG 3: THE FINALE

For all the lovers/fans of Anika and Blaze's relationship: Thank you all for following your favorite couple on this journey filled with love, suspense and drama. I hope you all enjoyed reading this series, because I sure loved writing it!

Thank You God, for guiding me and strengthening me always.

—

- Jouir de! -

Miss Jenesequa

BY MISS JENESEQUA

- Lustful Desires: Secrets, Sex & Lies
- Sex Ain't Better Than Love #1
- Sex Ain't Better Than Love #2
- Luvin' Your Man: Tales Of A Side Chick
- Down For My Baller #1
- Down For My Baller #2
- Bad For My Thug #1
- Bad For My Thug #2
- Bad For My Thug #3
- Addicted To My Thug

Miss Jenesequa

MISS JENESEQUA

BAD FOR MY THUG 3: THE FINALE

PROLOGUE

"Next time, slow down sir," the cop told him seriously, before handing him his ticket and walking away from his car.

Blaze rolled up his window before starting his engine and driving back on the road home. He was pissed that he had been caught speeding but the closer he got to Anika, the more he was quickly getting over it.

When pulling up to their condo, Blaze checked his iPhone only to see the text from Kareem telling him that he had arrived at Masika's. He planned to give his boy a call when he was settled in with Anika.

It didn't take long for him to be hot on his heels, out his car and opening the front door to enter his condo.

"Nika," he called out to her lovingly. "Daddy's home!"

He walked through their main living room, passed their kitchen and headed straight to the white door leading to their bedroom, only to see that it was ajar.

"Baby?"

After hearing no response, he went straight in, only to see complete darkness. Instead of switching on the light, he headed to the en-suite bathroom that had its light on. He figured she was in there peeing.

He figured wrong.

Upon entering, he noticed a device lying on the white bathroom sink and once moving closer to examine it, he noticed it to be a pregnancy test.

He suddenly picked it up, looking down to see the two lines on the white screen, telling him that it was positive.

If this was positive, then that meant... His baby was pregnant!

Blaze suddenly found himself grinning happily and wanting to scream out his joy, until he realized that Anika wasn't anywhere to be found.

It was when he headed back into the bedroom that his phone started to ring.

I just fucked yo' bitch in some Gucci flip flo-

"Sup Marq?" he greeted his boy, cutting off his ringtone as he flicked on the bedroom lights only to stare at the bright, large room with terror.

"Blaze, man, you won't believe this fuckin' shit! Kareem's been set up. We've been set up," he cried angrily.

Blaze remained speechless as he examined the bedroom that he shared with Anika.

He could see that the covers had been drug out, almost torn in some places, a lamp had been knocked over and a vase now lay on the floor in broken, shattered pieces.

"He's been shot over ten times! I've called the paramedics but… but I'on think he gon' make it B'."

Blaze's speechless mood suddenly cut off when he heard Marquise sniffling through the phone. "Kareem's been shot?! Who the fuck shot him?!"

"I'on know B'. I'm guessin' it's Leek," he said shakily. "He's bleedin' everywhere man and I can't find his fuckin' pulse."

Blaze couldn't believe what was going down right now. He was in Miami faced with some shit and on the phone with Marquise, who was in Atlanta faced with some shit!

"Masika missin' too! And Leek nowhere in fuckin' sight! But I know he did this shit. I just fuckin' know it."

"Anika's gone too," Blaze stated in disbelief, tiny tears forming in his eyes.

"Shit, what?!"

"She's been taken, Marq," Blaze voiced with nothing but fury in his deep voice. "My baby's pregnant and she been fuckin' kidnapped!"

"Man calm down, we gon' figure this shit out! I swear!" Marquise exclaimed.

"How can you expect for to me fuckin' calm down when my baby's gone!? She's fuckin' gone Marq! And now 'Reem fuckin' dyin' on us!" Tears were now rapidly falling down his cheeks.

"Man, I'm sorry, we gon' find her."

Blaze tried to remain as calm as he possibly could. He had to think. Who other than Leek was his enemy? Who could have been after his baby? Who was trying to ruin him? It was only a few short seconds later when he suddenly realized what he had failed to realize before.

He punched the wall in anger at the fact that he was slow in realizing this shit. How could he have been so damn stupid?

"I think I've figured who the fuck been workin' wit' Leek," Blaze snapped angrily, wiping his tears away with the back of his hand.

"Who?"

The man who his ex-fiancée had tried to seek help from. The man who the whole of Atlanta looked up to and admired. The man who had a lot of power when it came to the law. The man who had many people wrapped around his little finger. The man who had hurt his baby and now taken his baby.

"Jamal," Blaze stated sternly. "Jamal fuckin' Coleman."

CHAPTER 1 ~ MISSING YOU

"I am so fuckin' in love with you Nika and I'on wan' be with anotha chick but you. Ever," he voiced seriously before slowly leaving his seat.

Before Anika could try and stop him, he was already on one knee in front of her and pulling out a red box from behind him.

"Ever since I met you, I knew that you were the one for me. I knew that I was goin' to end up fallin' deeply in love with you. And you know I'on like doin' this corny shit, but I'ma do it for you, any day, any time. I love you so much Anika Scott," he announced lovingly as he lifted the small red ring box in the air towards her.

"You mean the world to me. You made me a better man and I just wan' you to be mine foreva baby. I wanna grow old with you and I wan' make lots and lots of cute ass babies with you."

Anika observed carefully as he opened the ring box and revealed the expensive, diamond piece of jewelry to her, making her eyes light up with shock and excitement.

"You the only woman I want Anika. You the only woman I need," he commented. "Anika Scott, will you become my Mrs. King?"

It took her a few minutes to respond but she did eventually.

"Yes," she whispered happily.

"Yes?" he questioned her with a happy smirk.

"Yes," she repeated. "Yes! Yes! Yes, Malik, I'll marry you."

Blaze had never been happier in his entire life. The fact that she had said yes and was willing to be his wife, had him jumping for joy.

He slid the silver diamond heart shaped ring down her finger before lifting her up in the air and spinning her playfully around off her feet.

"Malik!" she shouted playfully, "put me down."

"I love you, baby," he announced blissfully before branding his thick lips onto hers. The kiss was sweet, passionate and loving. Their tongues erotically danced, and Blaze found himself trying to express how much he loved and cherished his future wifey.

BAD FOR MY THUG 3: THE FINALE

That was two days ago. When Blaze had his baby right where she was supposed to be. By his side.

This was now.

Blaze reached for his AK-47 and stood up straight in his seat. He didn't care about the fact that he was going to go out in broad daylight with this large weapon by his side.

He was tired of this shit. He was tired of it all!

His love was still missing, and his boy was in a coma that seemed to not be improving. Blaze was tired of feeling heartbroken, pain and angry. He was tired of waiting. He was tired of sleeping alone. He was tired of crying. He was tired of it all. All he really wanted was for Anika to be safe, back with him, and Kareem to be out his damn coma. But what he wanted didn't seem to be coming anytime soon. So Blaze went with the second option.

He was going to find Jamal and Leek right this second and not waste a single moment, sending several bullets through their heads. All this waiting shit was just making him more frustrated and angry. He was done with waiting.

"Yo, B' what the... Nigga no!"

Blaze looked up into his best friend's eyes and only stared at him with fury. Marquise was now blocking his way as he stood in front of Anika's old apartment door.

"Blaze trust me, this ain't the answer."

The main reason why they were at Anika's apartment was because they figured that Jamal had been watching them. It made sense too, because with the amount of power he had due to his attorney status, he was able to make whatever he wanted to happen, happen. So the only place they could stay undetected was at Anika's old crib.

"So what is the answer then?!" Blaze questioned loudly, still holding his gun tightly to his side. "My baby's been taken and you think I'm just gon' to continue to sit here and wait? I need her back Marq! I need her back right fuckin' now!"

"And you will get her back, B', I promise," Marquise gently told his boy. "Just hang in there. We stick to the plan and everythin' gon' work out just fine."

"I'm tired of fuckin' waitin' Marq," Blaze snapped. "I just need to find her."

"So if I let you go out now, where the hell do you think you gon' find her? Where you think you gon' find Jamal and Leek's ass?"

Blaze had no idea, but he knew that trying was better than sitting around and waiting. He was tired of waiting. He was tired of being tired of waiting. All this shit had to stop. He needed everything to go back to the way it was before. He never wanted Anika to get involved in his lifestyle. She was just supposed to be protected by him. How could he fail at that one simple job?

"I'on know but I gotta do somethin'. You have no idea how I'm fuckin' feelin' right now Marq," Blaze informed Marquise rudely. "This shit hurts! I'm so fuckin' in love with her, I feel like I can't breathe! I need her... I need her... I need her back man..." Blaze's words continued to trail off sadly, as tears started leaving his eyes.

Marquise only stepped closer to his brother before embracing him tightly into his arms. He understood that Blaze was hurt, but going out in broad daylight with a dangerous weapon wasn't the answer. And he was sure that anyone to piss Blaze off in his path would feel his wrath.

"It's gonna be alright, bro," Marquise gently announced, patting his boy's back trying to comfort him. "We gon' find her, I promise."

CHAPTER 2 ~ REGRET

Looking at her love only brought sadness to her heart and tears to her eyes. As her tears slowly fell, she only looked on at his handsome face, peacefully at rest.

"I love you 'Reem," she announced. "And I know how much you love your sleep but I need you to wake up now baby... Okay?"

But even as she asked him nicely, he didn't move a muscle. Not a single sigh, eye twitch, muscle move, nothing. Only adding to Sadie's worry. He had been shot. Numerous times, in numerous locations, but by God's grace not a single bullet had managed to hit a major artery or organ. And for that, Sadie was grateful that her man hadn't been hit too severely. But he had still been hit.

Now, here he lay in a coma that seemed to not be improving. All Sadie wanted was for her man to wake up. She missed staring into those mesmerizing brown eyes of his, seeing that sexy gleaming smile and hearing that deep baritone of his.

"Reem... Please wake up," she cooed sweetly in his ear as she held his hand tightly in her own.

So far, he had only been in a coma for two days. The doctors said it could take up to six months for Kareem to wake up again, but Sadie couldn't wait that long for the love of her life to be back with her. She needed him now.

"I love you so much, and I just... I just need you back, fully awake with me," she softly spoke.

Kareem's coma wasn't the only bad thing to happen in her life right now. Sadie recently found out that her best friend, Anika had been taken while on vacation with her cousin.

Jamal Coleman had taken her in some sort of revenge plot to get back at Blaze. And to make things even worse, Anika was pregnant! She needed to be back home, where she was safe and sound with her future baby.

Sadie couldn't believe it all. Everything that was going on, was way too much for her to handle. She just didn't understand why everything was turning from bad to worse. All she wanted was for everything to go back to normal.

She missed Anika. She missed Kareem. All she wanted was the two people closest to her, to be safe and with her again. All this sadness was only continuing to break her heart every day; she didn't like crying in the middle of the night and waking up with dried tear stains on her face in the morning. She just wanted everything to go back to normal.

Sadie found herself suddenly bursting into tears and burying her head into Kareem's covered thigh. No amount of positive words that she could say to herself would be enough to make her feel any better right now. All she wanted was for her man to wake up. However, that only seemed to be a dream right about no-

"Uh... Sa... Sad..."

Sadie's teary eyes immediately popped open to the slight squeeze of a hand on hers, sounds of a deep voice, groaning and trying to speak. Her head quickly shot up and she was greeted by the handsome brown eyes of Kareem Smith.

More tears began to leave her eyes and before she knew it, she was pressing his red hospital button that would call his doctors and nurses to come check up on him.

To say she was happy would be an understatement right now. She was over the moon and all she could do was wipe away her tears, smile happily at her baby, and hope and pray that he was going to be okay.

"I missed you so much...Welcome back babe."

***

"...And he won't get off her couch or stop holding her pillow."

Blaze kept silent as he listened to Marquise's conversation with his Aunt Ari. He continued to hold onto Anika's favorite pillow and sniffed in her sweet scent that he missed so much.

"And he's just been sitting there?" Ari asked Marquise curiously, watching her nephew carefully.

"He's got up a few times, won't say much though," Marquise responded. "He's just been in this blank stare and tightly holdin' onto her pillow."

BAD FOR MY THUG 3: THE FINALE

He missed her. What was so hard about understanding that? Her pillow was the main thing that was around her, especially when she laid her pretty head on it to sleep at night. It was the best thing for him to be close to. And staying in her old apartment was the best option for him right now.

"And what's the plan to find her?" Ari queried.

"We've got a couple men lookin' 'round, we're currently unable to find the Lyons' new trap spots. They seemed to just have moved out of all the old ones. We have no idea where Jamal is currently residin' in Atlanta."

Ari kept silent for a few seconds, still watching Blaze as he stared off into space before announcing, "What if Jamal never left Miami the night he took Anika?"

"What you thinkin', Auntie?" Marquise questioned her, wondering what she was getting at.

"What if Jamal never left Miami the night he took Anika and just wanted you guys to think that? Maybe he's still there with her, just tryin' to buy some more time, you know, before decidin' on what to do next."

Blaze listened to her words carefully before agreeing with her. Jamal was probably still in Miami all this time with his baby! Blaze hoped it wasn't true but the more he thought about it, the more he was believing it.

"You might be right," Marquise said simply. "I'ma send a couple boys up to Miami tonight."

"No you ain't," Blaze suddenly intervened, surprising both his Aunt and Marq at his sudden input. "I'ma go up to Miami tonight. If he's got Anika with him, I'ma get her back." The idea of having Anika back right next to him in bed tonight, sounded so good to Blaze. So good. If he could make it happen, then he was going to make sure it happened, tonight.

"Malik, I don't think that's a good idea," Ari commented gently. "You need to stay here, just in case your boys find him he-"

"Fuck that!" Blaze shouted, cutting her off. "I'on wan' to stay."

"No Malik!" Ari shouted back, not happy at his rude tone towards her. "You're stayin' here. Where you can be calm, focus on finding

Jamal's new location and focus on your businesses. You ain't forget about all the businesses you need to run did you?"

"I gotta agree with Aunt Ari, B'," Marquise stated boldly. "You don't need to go to Miami, you need to stay here. You got too much shit going on ova here right now and we still lookin' for Jamal and Leek over here, regardless if they're in Miami."

Blaze wasn't trying to hear any of the bullshit ass words coming out of both his aunt's mouth and Marquise's. He was doing whatever the hell he wanted and if that meant going to Miami, then that's what the fuck he was going to do.

***

Heading back to Miami only resulted in Blaze's regret and sadness to come back. Seeing their hotel room and the locations they visited together, only resulted in bad thoughts to come back into his head.

He regretted the fact that he had taken Anika to Miami. If he hadn't taken her, she would have been safe and sound. Jamal wouldn't have even had a chance to take her away. There would have been no way that Blaze would have allowed it. He would have sent bullets flying, not caring about whether or not Jamal was going to be hurt. He would have sent that fool to his maker earlier than planned.

In Miami, Blaze didn't find Anika, Jamal or Leek. Blaze knew from the start that this was all his fault. He should have ended this from the very start. When Leek first had the courage to start trouble, he should have ended his life. If he had ended his life, then Leek wouldn't have found a new partner in Jamal. And Anika wouldn't have been taken.

All Blaze could do was sigh deeply as he flicked the next page in his club's profit books. The only place that he knew for sure that he could take his mind off Anika and the whole situation with Jamal and Leek, was if he went to his strip club to see how things were running without him.

He put people in charge to take care of it, but from time to time it was only right for him to check on how things were going in the business. From the profit books, everything seemed to be going really well.

No matter what shit people talked about strippers, they still loved paying money to see them dance. From the last six months alone, the profits of the club had skyrocketed through the roof. Now all Blaze could do was be satisfied that one side of his life was going well. Well, the legal side anyway. Next year he planned to open a restaurant. He had a love of cooking and food, so it was only right he opened a restaurant. But he wanted to make sure that when he opened it, Anika was right by his side making all the major decisions. After all, it was technically going to be all hers and named after her.

It was only when Blaze got to the last page in the book that his office door slowly pushed open.

Usually, he didn't let anyone enter unless they knocked and if they didn't knock, they got cursed the fuck out. But today, Blaze just wasn't in the mood.

He looked up only to see Candi standing in the doorway, staring at him carefully. She lifted her knuckle to the door, gently knocking before speaking.

"Can I come in B'?"

"You already in, ain't you?" he shot back.

"I guess..." She sheepishly walked in and shut the door behind her. "I haven't seen you in a minute. And I heard what happened to Anika... So I just wanted to make sure you were good."

Blaze began to stare her up and down. Candi was one of his best strippers at Cheetah Lounge so it wasn't a surprise to see her in a thin silver thong and a thin bikini bra that did a shitty job of hiding her tits away from him. But still, it was low-key weird for Blaze to see another woman other than Anika practically naked in front of him.

"I'll be good once I get her back," Blaze responded firmly.

"I'm sure you will be," Candi stated with a smile as she came to stand in front of his desk with her hands placed down in front of her. Blaze couldn't help but innocently stare at the top of her protruding breasts. "But if you ever need anythin' while she ain't 'round... I'm here."

Blaze gave her a stiff head nod, and before he knew it, she had turned around and was on her merry way out. Even as he watched the way her fat ass moved and that sexy switch in her hips, it didn't appease him as much as it used to.

It didn't matter how bad she was and how obvious it was she wanted Blaze to blow her back out. She wasn't Anika and she was never going to be Anika. And therefore, he could never go there and fuck her.

Ding!

Blaze suddenly looked down at his phone notification telling him of the text from Marquise.

South dope spot been hit. Lyons.

Blaze only angrily slammed his fists down on his mahogany desk before getting up and leaving.

He was going to make sure he killed every single one of those stupid fools and made them all suffer for his love being taken away from him. He was going to make them pay.

CHAPTER 3 ~ OLD IDOLS

To say Blaze was angry would be an understatement. He was fuming, beyond angry. As he listened to Marquise explain exactly what had happened at their dope spot up south being attacked, all he could literally see was red.

Knowing that the Lyons had attacked their dope spot the second time in the past six months, only added to the list of reasons for hating their entire squad. They were greedy, disrespectful and way too confident for no fucking reason! They weren't respected on the streets, but here they were still trying to prove a point. What point could they prove, other than the fact that they were dumb as hell?

Blaze knew he couldn't just take this disrespect anymore. He couldn't just sit around and think Jamal and Leek had one over on him. Yeah, they had Anika but they forgot about one thing: Blaze was a cold blooded murderer and he wasn't going to stop at anything until he brought both Leek and Jamal to their graves. He couldn't have them thinking they were getting away with shit. They wanted a war? Well they were definitely going to have one.

Two days later, Blaze found himself flying out to California to meet up with one of the very best in the drug game.

Jayceon Daniels.

He wasn't your typical thug ass nigga, especially as he loved wearing suits a lot, but he was still considered to be the best. He owned one of the best magazine outlets in the whole city of Los Angeles, and still had an army of soldiers moving weight for him on the streets every single day. He was the all-powerful Mr. Daniels and Blaze knew now more than ever he needed his help.

When being welcomed into his luxurious three-story mansion, Blaze knew that his baby would love to live in a house as big as this one. It was much bigger than Blaze's mansion back in Atlanta, leaving space for not just Anika's clothes and shoes, but for lots and lots and lots of little babies running around. The more he thought about it, the more he quickly began to become depressed. So he pushed the happy thoughts out his mind and focused on meeting Jayceon.

Jay's maid led him down a dimly lit corridor with pictures on the burgundy walls of Jayceon, his gorgeous wife Kristine, and their adorable female twins, before leading him to a large chestnut door and gesturing for Blaze to step inside.

Stepping inside resulted in Blaze's eyes to be exposed to the large beige colored room with various pieces of expensive furniture neatly arranged inside. It was when he stepped in deeper that he peeped Jayceon on the other side of the room in a large golden throne chair, smoking a Cuban cigar.

Jayceon's tense face immediately softened into a proud and optimistic expression, as he watched Blaze walk towards him.

"Long time no see, pretty boy," Jayceon spoke with a light laugh. The last time they had seen each other was ten years ago, when Blaze was seventeen and Jayceon was twenty-seven. It was that summer that Blaze decided with his boys that they were going to drop out of school and run the streets of Atlanta. To do that, Blaze knew he needed the expertise of one of the very best. So he got on a flight to Cali, burst into Jay's office and the rest was pretty much history. He taught Blaze all there was to know in a period of six months, shaping Blaze into one of the best drug dealers America had to offer. It was Jay's teaching that Blaze was able to pass onto his brothers and rule Knight Nation with them.

"Good to see you too, old nigga," Blaze sarcastically commented with a smirk.

"Now, what do I owe the pleasure of this visit? You know I'ma busy man Blaze."

"I know, I know, but I just had to see you Jay," Blaze responded with a sigh as he took a seat opposite his longtime friend, idol and mentor.

It didn't take Blaze very long to explain his current predicament to Jayceon. With it came Jay's head nods, raised brows and saddened expressions.

When he was done telling the whole situation, Jayceon gave him his honest opinion and advice. With it came help. Jayceon gave him an exclusive spot of his in Atlanta that was stocked with all the ammo and tools needed to help Blaze conquer his enemies. He also gave him a few added numbers of boys to help with the search of Anika and bringing Jamal to his grave. The only thing that confused the hell out of

Blaze was the attorney's number that Jay provided him with. He said that having an attorney on his side would bring him much victory and prosperity in the future, and that Blaze should use his new attorney to his advantage. Blaze didn't want the law snooping around into his business, but Jay assured him that if he gave the attorney a call, he would realize that he wasn't like that at all.

"Trust me pretty boy, things might seem bad now but once you've got yo' girl safe and sound, everything's gon' be good again, you'll see. And all those who wronged you will truly be punished."

Blaze could only thank his mentor and hope for the very best. He needed his woman back more than ever. He just prayed that her and their unborn baby were hanging in there as best as they could.

***

"I thought you were going to die."

Kareem looked down at his Queen's unhappy facial expression, only starting to feel unhappy because of her unhappiness.

"Babe, don't say that," he told her gently, reaching for her hand that rested on his thigh. Kareem stared deeply into her teary eyes and just decided to let her speak. It was clear she wanted to get some things off her chest.

"I thought you were going to die and leave me here all alone Kareem," she continued. "I just remember seeing you there and... and... thinking you were gone."

"I'm back now, Sadie," he explained, slowly lifting her hand to his lips. "And I swear I ain't neva gon' leave you like that again. I promise." He lovingly kissed her hand, trying to get her to lighten up. He didn't want her reminiscing on old stuff that didn't matter anymore. What mattered was them moving on together towards their happy future.

"I love you Sadie and I just want us to be together foreva, in love and makin' lots of babies. You the only woman I want', I swear I'on want no one else."

"What are you tryin' to say, 'Reem?" Sadie curiously asked, wanting to know what he was getting at.

"I know where we are right now ain't the best time to be doin' this but..." His words trailed off as he took a deep breath and tried to calm his nerves. There wasn't a single doubt in his mind that Sadie was the one for him. The one he needed to be with. He wanted to make her his wife.

However, just as he plucked up the courage to propose to her, Kareem's hospital door suddenly swung open and in stepped the woman he thought he would never ever see again.

Sadie turned to the open door only to see a beautiful woman, dressed in all black and now smiling happily at Kareem. She was wearing what looked like an expensive leather jacket, black leggings and black Louboutins.

Sadie couldn't help but stare at her with annoyance. What the hell was she doing over here wearing all black? This wasn't a funeral.

"K," she called out to him.

"Satin?"

From the way Kareem was now looking at this chick and the way she was looking back at him, Sadie knew that wherever they knew each other from, it was going to piss her the fuck off.

***

Anika wanted to die.

She would rather die than be kept here in this hell hole. She hated being here. She would rather die than being away from her man, her best friend and her future husband. She missed him now more than ever, and knowing that she was carrying his seed and he wasn't able to protect the both of them, was breaking her heart each day.

Looking across the decrepit room she sat in, Anika could see Masika's back facing the wall and her eyes tightly shut. Whether she was awake or asleep, Anika didn't care. She hated Masika and she had a strong feeling that it was all her fault that they were both being kept against their will in this abandoned warehouse.

Anika looked down at her left hand, eyeing the expensive ring that Blaze had proposed to her with, the night she was taken. It was the only thing that managed to keep her sane each day. Knowing that she belonged to her man and nobody else, was what was keeping her happy. Knowing that he loved and cherished her.

Even though Anika was given food, new clothes and a chance to wash daily, she was still being treated badly. She couldn't speak unless being spoken to, Jamal's exact orders, and not even a single ounce of fresh light had touched her skin since being in Miami with Malik.

BAD FOR MY THUG 3: THE FINALE

She just wanted to go home. She was tired of this. She knew that if Blaze didn't come to rescue her soon, bad things would happen. Bad things involving her and her baby's well-being.

Jamal and Leek had been talking a lot, and Anika had managed to catch a few words whenever she could. She was sure Masika had too. The men had talked about moving them, killing Masika, chopping Anika's finger off so they could send it to Blaze, and even using Anika as bait to trap Blaze and murder him.

Anika knew that whatever they were planning, she would have to use every fiber of her being to stop their plans. She couldn't let them ruin her man. If she had to die trying to save the one she loved more than anything, then so be it.

Her only concern right now was getting out of here so she could check up on her baby. She wasn't sure if things were good. Especially since she hadn't been eating well and she had been experiencing a few stomach cramps lately. She just prayed that she wasn't losing the one thing that she was looking forward to bringing into the world.

Malik's seed.

Masika only kept her eyes shut and tried to shake off all the emotions that were trying to circulate through her head. She didn't want to think about the negative shit anymore. She had already done that. After almost being beaten to death by Leek, she knew there was nothing worth living for other than her man, Blaze.

She knew that he was probably trying his hardest to find Anika and finding Anika would result in him finding her. And she would be free.

But she also knew that it must have been hard. If it was taking this long for him to find them, the shit must have been pretty hard.

That's why Masika knew she needed to come up with a plan to lead Blaze to where she was. She would deal with getting rid of Anika later, but for now, it was imperative that Masika found a way to get Blaze to know about her whereabouts.

If only she could figure out a way to charge her dead phone... That way she could contact Blaze and give him an idea of where she was. She wasn't sure of the exact location but she was sure that she had heard Leek and his partner, Jamal, discuss the area before.

North Druid Hills.

MISS JENESEQUA

One text to Blaze and she was sure that he would be here sooner than later.

CHAPTER 4 ~ BONDED BROTHERS

"A'ight, we can do this the hard way or the easy way," Marquise explained simply as he sat down on the back of the chair, facing Tone with a tense expression. "I've already told you 'bout my boy here bein' very angry 'bout Leek fuckin' with his girl, but I, on the other hand, am willin' to do this calmly and listen to what you have to tell us today."

Blaze stood still against the wall as he watched Marquise talk to Tone. Tone had been found by a couple of their boys, downtown at Marquise's local night club.

The fact that Tone had so confidently and easily been chilling at Marquise's local night club, pissed Blaze off beyond a point of no return. He was already waking up every single day and finding himself pissed at life. Pissed because of all the predicaments he was in already. All because of Jamal and Leek.

"I ain't gon' say shit!" Tone suddenly shouted boldly, only adding to Blaze's annoyance. He badly wanted to walk towards where Tone sat and fuck him up in the worst possible way. Instead, he remained silent and still, waiting for Marquise's attempts to get the truth out of Tone, to be over.

"You ain't gon' say shit?" Marquise queried curiously, gently rubbing on his freshly shaved chin with a smirk. "You really think that sayin' nothin' is the best thing to do right now nigga?"

"The Lyons will forever rule. We ain't scared of you Knights no more, especially since we got all the ammo, protection and power we need now," Tone responded proudly.

Ammo, protection and power? Blaze couldn't help but chuckle in his head at Tone's silly words. They really thought that they were the shit compared to Knight Nation. Jamal must have been filling their heads with complete lies to get them to be on his team. There was no way that they were as powerful as they thought they were. Not when Blaze was currently after them. They had already caught one of their men slipping, so it would only be a matter of days before Blaze caught the rest of them slipping.

"And who's givin' you all this fuckin' power nigga? Who exactly do you believe is gon' protect you from us?" Marquise asked Tone in a firm tone, staring deeply into his eyes.

Tone decided to keep silent and not bother answering his questions. He didn't seem as confident anymore to speak.

"If you so protected, how come we managed to catch you slippin' and take you so easily? And better yet, ain't no one come to find yo' dumb ass yet," Marquise announced. "So all powerful Tone, where exactly is yo' protection at now? You think they comin' to get you anytime soon?"

Blaze knew exactly what Marquise was doing. He was questioning Tone, not necessarily expecting him to answer, but making sure that the questions got him to really think and evaluate his spot with his squad. If he managed to think hard enough, he would realize that there wasn't a single person coming for him. And that would make him crack, telling them all the things they needed to know. Blaze hoped that for his sake, he cracked or else he was going to make him crack by force.

"They gon' come for me," Tone mumbled quietly.

"What'chu say?" Marquise loudly questioned, not quite hearing him.

"They gon' come for me!" he shouted. "They will!"

Marquise kept silent at his words before shaking his head in disappointment at Tone. "See... I was givin' you a huge opportunity to save yo'self. Now I see that you so fuckin' retarded and brainwashed, that you can't see that no one is comin' to save you! You stayin' here for as long as we need you to stay here. Ain't no one comin' fool."

"...They're co-"

"And now that you couldn't let me handle things the easy way, you gon' feel the hard way. The way that you really don't want to feel. Remember I told you 'bout my boy?" Marquise pointed behind him, causing Tone to stare directly into Blaze's steely, grey eyes that were filled with fury and a promise of revenge. "He's gon' handle you now." With saying that, Marquise got up from his seat and turned around to face Blaze.

"He's all yours, B'."

BAD FOR MY THUG 3: THE FINALE

Within a matter of seconds, Blaze was standing by the chair that Marq had been sitting in and quickly picked it up. He stared into Tone's frightened, teary eyes, waiting to see if he was willing to say anything to save himself before Blaze begun his tortures. However, Tone only kept quiet and looked up with fear at Blaze.

So Blaze begun.

He lifted the chair up in the air before violently whacking it down onto Tone's hard head, a loud thud sounding from the impact.

All he could do was yell out in pain but he couldn't move, or try to run. Especially with his hands and legs tied to the wooden chair that he was forced to sit in.

Seeing that the first hit didn't do too much damage, Blaze decided to keep going.

Up and down he lifted the chair, making each hit harder than the one before. Marquise even found himself turning away to stop looking at the scene. He knew his brother was angry but damn... The nigga was going harder and harder by the minute.

Violently and determinedly, Blaze continued to swing the metal chair up and down over Tone's head. Even with the amount of blood that was now on the legs of the chair, the amount of blood that covered the side of Tone's head...

He didn't stop.

"You still ain't gon' fuckin' talk?!" Blaze crazily fumed, only increasing the speeds of his aggressive hits with the metal chair. "Where the fuck is Leek at?!"

The more he hit, the more blood was gushing out from Tone's head. Blaze didn't care though. He was so angry. So angry. And the more he continued to use the metal legs to hit on Tone, the easier he began to feel. He was finally putting all that pent up anger of losing Anika, into something. This was the only thing that he knew would make him happy now.

"Stupid ass niggas, really think I'm gon' let y'all get away with this shit," Blaze declared through gritted teeth, still whacking and hitting on Tone's head and body with the metal chair.

The smell of blood had filled the warehouse room, but Blaze still didn't care. Up. Down. He continued to use the chair as his beating weapon against Tone. The harder he hit, the better it felt.

MISS JENESEQUA

It was only five minutes later when Blaze heard a cracking noise against Tone's skull, that he suddenly stopped. Tone's head was now hanging down towards the floor and he was no longer screaming or yelling. He was frozen and when Blaze inched closer to lift his head up, he noticed the way it loosely held up and just dropped back down.

Blaze had killed him.

Marquise suddenly turned around noticing the sounds of metal hitting a head had stopped and when he sauntered closer to where Blaze stood, he looked down at Tone's lifeless body.

Was his plan to kill Tone or just to get him shook enough to speak? Either way, Tone was dead and Blaze still knew nothing about where Anika was, where Leek was or where Jamal was. What the hell had he just done?

"I'ma call some of the boys to come clean this shit up," Marq spoke, breaking Blaze out of his trance. "We should probably get goin'. We gotta handle a few deliveries comin' through today."

Blaze kept silent and just looked regretfully at Tone's dead body. He had killed numerous niggas before, but this one in particular hurt. Mostly because of the fact that this was his one step closer to getting Anika back and he had just blown it.

Ding!

Blaze looked at Marquise as he quickly began to look at his phone. He carefully watched as Marq's hazel eyes widened with surprise and a large smile grew on his lips.

"What's up?" Blaze asked, wondering why he looked happy all of a sudden.

"You get a text from Sadie?"

Blaze shook his head no.

"Check yo' phone. I'm sure she texted you."

Blaze followed his friend's orders and grabbed his phone from his back pocket. He had put his phone on do not disturb, so he wouldn't get distracted while handling business. When pressing on his home screen button, he was greeted to the numerous texts and missed calls from Sadie. One text in particular stood out to him.

Kareem's awake.

***

BAD FOR MY THUG 3: THE FINALE

Blaze had never been happier this entire week. Ever since losing Anika, he had felt like his entire happiness had been sucked out of him. She had taken it all with her. But now, knowing that his boy was awake was bringing joy to his heart.

As Blaze and Marquise excitedly walked through the hospital wards to Kareem's room, they could hear the loud shouts of two female voices.

One that sounded extremely like Sadie's and one that sounded vaguely familiar. But Blaze found himself struggling to put a name or face to the voice in his head.

"Just leave bitch!"

"No, I won't fucking leave. K wants me here!"

"No he doesn't want you here! Who the hell are you?"

"K, just tell her who I am already, I'm tired of hearing this fool scream and shout."

"Scream and shout?! Oh bitch, don't worry, I'll show you more than scream and shout in a minute."

It was only when they quickly burst through into Kareem's hospital room, when they saw what the commotion was all about.

Kareem was wide awake, frustrated until he saw Blaze and Marquise enter the room. Near Kareem's bed, stood Sadie shouting across the room.

Blaze took a glance to the right only to see who exactly Sadie was shouting at and who was shouting right back.

"Satin?" Blaze said, surprised and shocked to see her after all these years.

"Who the fuck is this bitch?! Why the hell are y'all acting surprised now that y'all see her?! Who is she 'Reem?!"

Everyone kept silent and just looked on at the gorgeous woman, standing proudly in the corner with a smirk on her face.

"So ain't none of you niggas gonna say hello to your sister-in-law?" Satin questioned Blaze and Marquise curiously.

"Sister-in-law?" Sadie asked rudely. "What the fuck does she mean 'Reem?"

"That's right bitch," Satin responded happily. "They classify themselves as brothers, right? So I'm their sister-in-law."

"And how the fuck are you their sister-in-law, you dumb ho-"

"I'm Kareem's wife," Satin snapped, interrupting Sadie. "That's how."

All an annoyed and shocked Sadie could do was suddenly keep silent at her words.

"Kareem and I are married and have been for the last five years now."

CHAPTER 5 ~ REALIZATIONS

"But why are you here Satin?" Blaze piped up, seeing that his cousin was now upset and not bothering to say anything else. He wanted to get the information that she wanted from the start. Seeing Sadie upset wasn't something he liked to see at all.

"I'm back because Kareem called me here."

"That true 'Reem?" Marq turned to Kareem, who lay with a guilty expression as he watched Sadie. Sadie wasn't looking at him though. She was still looking at Satin with shock and disbelief. Blaze knew that he would have to keep his eye on her. If she wanted to swing on Satin, she was going to do it regardless of the two thugs that stood in her way.

Kareem nodded sheepishly, much to Sadie's annoyance.

"Oh, so now you can't speak nigga?" Sadie turned to face him with a rude expression fixed upon her pretty face. "No hablas Inglés ahora?! *(Do you not speak English now?)* Speak up nigga! You the one that called her here, right?!"

"Chill Sadie," Blaze said.

"No I ain't gon' chill!" Sadie fumed. "Why would he call her here?"

"He never said," Satin explained. "He just said he wanted to see me in person and talk, which was about a few weeks ago. I'm guessing he wanted to talk about us and that's why I came. We separated after our first year of marriage, but I'm guessing that he wants to get back together now. I love him still and I want him back."

"Well news flash for you bitch," Sadie began with the utmost confidence. "He doesn't want you anymore. He's happy with someone else right now, so you just gonna have to let him go."

"Okay, and if you're so happy Kareem, tell me you don't want me anymore and I'll go. I'll never bother you again," Satin announced.

"Cool," Sadie agreed happily. "He's gonna tell you, he's perfectly fine with me. Go ahead, tell her babe."

Sadie waited patiently, waiting expectantly for Kareem to say the words that she wanted to hear. She kept staring at Satin with pride until a few seconds passed and Kareem had yet to speak.

"Reem, tell her," Sadie pushed, looking at him strangely. What was he playing at? All he had to do was say that he wanted to be with Sadie and Satin would be on her merry way to wherever the hell she came from.

"See? He doesn't want me to leave," Satin commented. "So I think the real person who should leave here, is you."

Sadie couldn't believe what she wasn't hearing right now. This nigga was just going to lay on this bed and not declare his love for her, right now in front of his wife. She couldn't believe it. The same regret and fear she had when she first let him have her was coming back, and she knew that it was all too good to be true.

He had just been a waste of time.

Quickly, Sadie picked up her bag and ran out the hospital room, ignoring Kareem's pleas for her to stay.

"Baby, don't go! Stay, please! Sadie!"

Why the hell would she stay, when he clearly didn't want her the way she thought he did. He had just been a mistake it now seemed. If he truly loved her like he claimed he did, then why was it so hard for him to claim her in front of his wife?

Sadie couldn't even believe that he was married. Why hadn't he told her that from the start? She would have understood that he was separated but no, he hadn't said a word. Not a damn word!

Blaze was confused. He looked at Kareem strangely and slowly becoming pissed again because at the fact that Sadie was upset. He would have to check up on her later though.

"Satin, leave," Blaze suddenly snapped.

"What? No wh-"

"I ain't gon' tell you again."

Satin slowly walked towards the exit before saying, "I'll be outside if you need be 'Reem." And then she left.

Kareem could tell by the way Blaze was staring at him, sending daggers his way that he was pissed, but he knew he could quickly rectify the issue. Well he hoped.

"Blaze, I can exp-"

"Don't think that because yo' ass is on this bed that I can't beat yo' ass up later," he voiced tensely, sauntering closer to Kareem's bedside.

"B', I can explain," Kareem stated in an assuring tone.

"Start explain', nigga," Marquise ordered, moving closer to Kareem's bedside too.

"I love Sadie, y'all know I do."

"So why ain't you tell Satin to leave just now?" Blaze asked.

"I need Satin right now," Kareem explained simply.

"And why's that?" Marq queried.

"I'm tryna propose to Sadie," Kareem said. "I was tryna do it earlier in fact, but Satin came in and interrupted a nigga."

"And how the hell do you expect to marry my cousin when yo' ass is already married?"

"That's why I need Satin, B'. We gotta get a divorce. I should have done that shit ages ago, but you boys know how I was before."

"Yeah, we know," Marquise answered with a chuckle. "Fuckin' anythin' with a pussy and a fat ass."

"Now I'm a changed man," Kareem promised. "And I want Sadie to be my wifey, foreva. But I'on know how to break it to Satin yet. I called her up here weeks ago, but she didn't seem to want to come at first. Now she's here and she's got the wrong idea 'bout what I want from her. I want' a divorce, but I gotta break it to her slowly or she could just refuse me. Then how the hell am I 'posed to marry the love of my life?"

"We'll make sure she won't refuse you, lover boy," Blaze replied firmly.

"Nah B', no funny business. She gotta do this on her own accord," Reem explained. "It's her signature that's goin' on the document."

"Well, whateva the fuck you need to do, do it nigga," Blaze said in a tense tone. "I'on want you to fuck around with Sadie's emotions. You know how sensitive she gets and shit. And I warned you before not to fuck up nigga."

"Trust me, I know man, I know… I won't fuck up. I just gotta a little confused but I want her only."

"Good," Blaze voiced. "Glad to have you back nigga."

"Glad to be back," Kareem stated with a deep sigh. "I swear if it wasn't for me not thinkin' straight that night, shit wouldn't be like this. Sadie told me about Anika and Jamal, I'm sorry B'."

"Hey, it's not yo' fault, nigga," Blaze assured him. "Our main focus right now is findin' out where Leek and Jamal got her at."

"Don't forget Masika," Kareem added. "I'm sure she's part of it. That bitch definitely set me up. Before I knew it I was bein' led straight into a trap."

"So she just led you to the room where Leek was?" Marquise queried.

"Yeah man," Kareem said with a nod. "She made me believe that he was asleep after them fuckin'. But turns out the nigga was wide awake and before I knew it, he was sending bullets straight my way. Before I could even think 'bout shootin' back or runnin', this nigga was shooting at all directions through me."

"So Masika set you up because Leek told her to, so you think she's part of the whole plot against kidnappin' Anika?"

Blaze reminded silent, contemplating on Marquise's words for a bit. Masika seemed happy to help them get Leek, but now thinking about it, she was probably working with them the whole time just pretending not to. It made sense too. She was just a snake and Blaze knew that if he ever saw her again, he was going to send one bullet straight through her heart as punishment for crossing him.

After all they had been through together, he would have never imagined her trying to cross him. She knew him well. She knew what he was capable of. So why risk getting in trouble, just to end up dead? She was now officially part of his enemy list and he was going to make her, Leek and Jamal all pay.

"Yeah, I think so," responded Blaze. "Makes sense. She was probably just feedin' them information and tryin' to get the right time to set one of us up. Now that I think about it, Kareem ain't trust her ass from the start. I should have listened to you, nigga."

"It's all in the past B'," Kareem explained. "We just gotta focus on the future now. Findin' Anika and killin' all those fools."

"Yeah... And my baby's pregnant too. I need her back safe and sound."

BAD FOR MY THUG 3: THE FINALE

"She's pregnant?" Kareem asked with surprise. "Congrats nigga."

"Thanks," Blaze said sadly.

"We gon' find her, don't worry B," Marquise promised. "All our boys are out lookin', even got a few feds on our side too, and Jayceon got us covered."

"Oh word? Jayceon helpin' us too?"

"Yeah, I flew out to Cali and went to go see him a few days ago," Blaze responded, knowing that Kareem wasn't aware of his visit to Jay. "He gave us a new dope spot, ammo, soldiers and an attorney."

"An attorney?" Reem asked, confused.

"Yeah, he said somethin' 'bout havin' an attorney on our side. It'll help or some shit like that."

"I hope so," Kareem replied with a shrug. "We really don't need the law sniffin' into our shit right now."

"They won't," Blaze explained. "Jay promised the attorney ain't like that. He on our side."

"Well as long as this can all help towards gettin' back Anika, findin' Masika, Leek and Jamal, then I ain't got a problem with it," Kareem declared. "...Speakin' of Masika..." Kareem slowly turned to the side of his bed only to reach for his iPhone that sat on the cabinet near him.

"I just remembered the bitch texted me some dodgy shit a few hours ago."

"What?" Blaze's eyes widened with suspicion.

"What she say?" Marquise wondered.

Kareem lifted his bright phone screen towards Blaze. Blaze grabbed the phone only to see the text sent from Masika.

'NDH.'

"NDH?" Blaze spoke out loud, taking one last glance at the text before passing it to Marquise. "NDH? The fuck that mean?"

"I have no clue," Kareem said. "As you can see I texted her back, even tried callin' but I got sent straight to voicemail."

"It must stand for some shit," Marquise suggested. "You think she's tryna tell us somethin'?"

"It seems like it," Blaze answered with a frown. "Maybe she didn't want to set you up that night 'Reem, but Leek made her. How did she seem that night when you first saw her?"

"From what I can remember, she looked teary eyed and her voice was quite hoarse. I thought it was maybe because of the fact that her and Leek had been fuckin' all night."

"Or maybe he had hurt her and she was screamin'?" Marquise continued to wonder.

"Shit!" Blaze yelled with the sudden realization of something. "I think she's with Anika. Leek must have found out she was workin' with us."

Now that they all thought about it, it all made sense. Leek probably discovered that Masika was working with them and decided to make her set up Kareem. Now she was being kept with Anika.

"A'ight, so now we know that she's not exactly a snake. What the hell does NDH stand for?"

"I'on know, Marq," Blaze answered. "All I know is that it must be a clue."

"This bitch got us goin' like we on some fuckin' adventure show," Kareem commented angrily. "Why ain't she just type the whole thing out?"

"No idea... But we just need to think real hard 'bout what NDH could stand for. It's probably our key to findin' Anika."

The boys knew that NDH was their way to Anika, and right now all they could do was think in silence and try to become unconfused by Masika's mysterious text.

CHAPTER 6 ~ NORTH DRUID HILLS

Masika almost wanted to scream out all her anger until it all left her system, but she quickly remembered where she was.

Sending a quick text to Kareem had proved to be successful, but in the process, fatal. She had managed to sneak out to Leek's office while Jamal and Leek had gone out somewhere, and found a charging port for her phone. They had forgotten to lock the room that she and Anika were being forced to stay in and to say that she was glad was an understatement. She was over the moon!

That didn't mean that they hadn't locked up the rest of the building, because Masika had checked and they had. But nonetheless, she had managed to leave the charging plug in her phone, until it lit up her phone screen so that it could switch on. Then she suddenly heard the unlocking of the front main door and quickly ran back into the room where Anika was.

She didn't bother telling Anika what she was doing. They didn't really talk to one another at all, other than giving each other glances and dirty looks. Masika could sense that Anika didn't like her and she was cool with that, because she hated Anika. She knew Anika would find out soon enough what she had been up to, when Blaze came busting through that door and came to rescue them both.

When her phone had fully switched on, she saw it had two percent and she panicked. She knew that attempting to call Blaze would fail because the battery would quickly drain because of the incoming connection to another phone. So she quickly went to her messages and sent a text to the last number she had texted before shit went left.

Kareem's.

When clicking on their message, her phone battery went to 1% and she knew that it was now or never. So she quickly typed the initials of the place that she heard Leek talking about a few days ago to someone on the phone. NDH. North Druid Hills.

And as soon as she had pressed send, her smartphone died.

MISS JENESEQUA

All she could do was pray that Kareem was okay and he was not dead. She was fully aware of Leek shooting him frantically, and could not forget the amount of blood that she saw gushing out of him.

She only prayed and hoped that he was alive for her sake. He had to figure out what NDH stood for and tell Blaze. He was now her only way out of here.

***

A week later and Kareem was feeling better than ever, despite his nurses and doctor advising him to stay in the hospital for an additional two weeks. Kareem strongly disagreed. He wasn't about to stay down on that bed any longer, when he had shit to do.

Masika's text had been driving him crazy all week, and he was still trying to figure out what it meant. And to top it all off, he was still trying to get through to Sadie but she had blocked his calls. So he knew exactly what he had to do.

He called for an Uber to come pick him up from the hospital, since his car was still at Masika's crib after the incident. Now he was heading straight to Sadie's crib, hoping she would let him in.

He hadn't expected to see Satin pop up at the hospital. He wasn't even sure how she had known he would be there, but she had found out. She had always been such a smart girl. She must have guessed he was in trouble when she popped up at his crib and seen that he wasn't around.

Satin used to be the love of Kareem's life. That's the only reason why he agreed to marry her all those years ago, when she said she wanted him to be hers forever. He was willing to do anything for her, including make a ton of babies with her and be hers.

But she had played him.

In reality, all she really wanted was the money and with the money, she wanted clothes, shoes, bags, cars and a big mansion.

Kareem thought that giving her everything she wanted would show her how much he loved her, but it turned out she never really loved him. She was just using him for the dollars, to get what she wanted in life, and fucking other niggas on the side. So to hear her say she loved him still, was a shock for Kareem.

Kareem would never forget the day he came home and saw her laid out naked on their bed, asleep. He figured she was waiting for him but when he saw the numerous condoms on the floor around their bed and the semen splattered on her breasts, stomach and pussy, he knew that she had been sneaking around on him.

The dirty bitch had had the audacity to fuck another dude on their bed, too! It angered 'Reem so much, he almost beat the living daylights out of her that day, but he knew he wasn't no woman beater. So he kicked her ass out.

Now she was back, but confused with the reason of why he wanted her here. He just needed her to agree to the divorce, sign the papers, and she would be out of his life for good. He would give her money if she needed it, just to make sure that she stayed well away from him and Sadie.

When finally arriving at Sadie's, Kareem was quickly ran up the stairs in his J's to Sadie's apartment floor. He had his copy of her keys in his back pocket and once standing in front of her oak door, he pulled them out and began opening the door.

Much to his anger though, she had changed the locks and he wasn't able to enter as easily as he thought he would. The fact that she had changed the locks so quickly made him unhappy. He didn't like the fact that she thought she was getting rid of him so easily.

So he decided to knock, hoping she would at least come to the door and talk to him.

"Sadie!" he called out to her, knocking loudly. "Let me in!"

"No fool!" she shouted on the other side of the door. "Go to your hoe!"

"Sadie, please! Let me in!" he continued to shout, banging loudly on her door. A few of her neighbors were beginning to come out their homes to see what the noise was all about. But once they saw Kareem glaring rudely at them, they went straight back inside.

"I'm not letting you in, so go away nigga!" Sadie fumed, holding her ground and determined not to let him in. Not after he had done her wrong and hurt her so badly.

"Please let me in, baby! I love you."

"No you don't," she spat. "You couldn't even tell me that in front of that bitch, so you clearly don't love me."

"I do, Sadie," he promised. "Just let me in so a nigga can explain."

"No! Go away!"

Seeing that his gentle ways weren't working, Kareem knew that he would have to change tactics. Clearly, she thought that she could easily push him away. Well, she thought wrong.

"Let me in Sadie," he voiced firmly.

"No, go aw-"

"I ain't gon' ask you again, Sadie. Let me in."

"And what exactly do you think gon' happen if you ask me again? You're the one on the other side of the door, fool."

"You really wanna find out what's gon' happen if I ask you again?"

"Yes I do," Sadie said proudly.

"No you don't," he snapped. "Because you won't have a front door no more."

Sadie's eyes widened with fear. "You wouldn't dare."

"Try me," he stated with a smirk, knowing that he had found a way in.

"Go ahead then! Break down the door!"

"You really don't want that to happen Sadie," he explained before suddenly kicking on her door.

Sadie jumped at the sound of the loud bang and the vibrations of her door moving against his hard kick.

"Yo' door ain't even that strong. I'd say I could kick that shit down in a few sec..." His words quickly trailed off once he heard the unlocking of her door and saw that she had opened it for him.

"Say what you need to say and get the fuck out," she retorted before turning around to walk away from him. But as soon as he stepped inside her apartment, he grabbed her arm and pulled her closer towards him.

"Uh-uh, you ain't runnin' away that easily," he demanded, shutting her door close with his foot before pulling her roughly against the door. She suddenly looked down away from him, trying to hide how turned on she was because of him, but she knew he still knew.

"Look at me, Sadie."

Still she looked down, unable to think straight at how close his hard body was pressed up against hers. She could smell his sexy, spicy masculine scent and it was turning her on faster and faster by the second. All she wanted to do was jump him.

"I ain't gon' tell yo' ass again, Sadie."

She hated when he did that. But loved it also; when he threatened to do something if she didn't do what he wanted. His aggressive but gentle nature was one that she would never stop loving.

"Look at me," he ordered and she quickly lifted her head up to stare up into his brown mesmerizing eyes. "I love yo' ass and you the only one I want to be with."

"Then why di-"

"Did I say you should start speakin'?"

"No, bu-"

"Then don't speak," he retorted, lifting his hands to the sides of her waist. "You the only one I want Sadie. Fuck Satin, she's not important. She don't mean shit to me no more. Not the way you mean to me. A'ight?"

Sadie reluctantly nodded.

"Speak," he prompted her with a small smile. "I wanna hear you say you forgive me and you love me."

"I... I don't forgive you Kareem."

"What the fuck, why not?" he asked, feeling his mind fill with fury.

"Because... You failed to tell her that you loved me 'Reem!"

Kareem sighed deeply before responding, "I know bae. I'm so-"

"If you don't love me, then I suggest you turn around and leave."

"And why the fuck would I do that when I want to be with you Sadie?" He asked her rudely.

"Well it sure don't seem like you love me. I'm mean you found it so hard to say earlier in front of that bitch," she retorted.

"Sadie, I love you. And I'm sorry I didn't sa-"

She quickly cut him off, "Would you have told me you were married?"

"You know I'm married now don't you?"

"Would you have told me if she hadn't come?" Sadie questioned suspiciously, arching a brow at him.

"Yea', I would have," he promised sweetly. "How could I have not told you, when I plan to make you wifey one day?"

"You do?"

"Of course I do baby," he said. "When the time is right, I promise shorty, I'ma make you Mrs. Smith."

Sadie couldn't help but light up with happiness at his words, and she lifted herself up on the balls of her feet so she could brand her lips onto his.

Kareem had only now realized that they hadn't really managed to kiss properly once he had woken up from his coma. And now with that big bulge growing in his pants, he knew how many days it had been since they last made love.

Their tongues began to dance and before she knew it, Sadie was up on her feet and legs securely wrapped around Kareem's torso, as he led the way to her bedroom.

"I've... missed you so... much daddy," Sadie announced lustfully in between their heated kiss.

"Hmmm," Kareem gently groaned, feeling her slightly rub on his erection. "You gon'... show me... just how much?"

"Yes daddy... Mmmm..." She then tilted her head to the side, offering her neck to the teasing appeal of Kareem's lips, sliding her fingers through his picky hair. "Reem..." She sighed deeply. Enjoying the feel of his thick, soft lips on her neck.

He then stopped kissing on her neck and suddenly threw her onto her king size California double lilac bed.

"I missed that pussy so much, baby," Kareem announced sexily, slowly stripping in front of her.

"I missed that dick even more daddy," Sadie replied with a bite to her lips as she watched her man strip for her.

Once that hot, hard muscular body was revealed to her after all these days, Sadie found herself heating up with desire and anticipation for Kareem.

BAD FOR MY THUG 3: THE FINALE

Oh my... He looks so good! I just want to eat him all up. Kiss on every single one of those abs, rub on his warm skin and keep kissing on his tattoos all night.

She couldn't wait to show him just how much she had missed him.

***

Blaze was left to do nothing, but wait. Even though he was tired of waiting, he knew right now, waiting was the best thing for him to do. There was no point in trying to rush shit, it was better it happened with time. He just had to wait and hope for the best.

So, here he sat in his office, checking the books again and trying to take his mind off how much he missed his baby.

It wasn't working though. He found himself laying back against his chair, shutting his eyes and thinking about Anika.

Everything about her he was trying his hardest to forget, because the more he remembered, the more hurt he was. However, shit wasn't working. Because all he could think about was her.

Her pretty face, her smile, those gorgeous eyes, that sweet laugh, that cute nose, those soft lips and that... that tight, tight, tight pussy of hers.

Damn he missed her. He missed kissing all over her body and kissing her lips 'til he couldn't breathe. He missed making love to her, he missed all the shit they used to do around midnight, all the freaky things they used to do together, their conversations, their private jokes... everything.

He imagined her warm hands, massaging his skin and making him feel good. He imagined her gently kissing his cheeks, and moving her lips onto his. She was such a good kisser. She knew how to do him so well, make their tongues dance so passionately together. Blaze even found himself moving his hands to her waist during their heated make out session. He moved his hands down her waist and to her back, only to slowly slide down to her ass.

Shit! Even feeling on her juicy flesh and realizing that she was only wearing a thong right now had him wanting to almost bust in his pants. And with the way she was now sitting on his lap, directly on his growing dick, was only driving him crazy.

Why was this dream so real and vivid? Why could he feel how wet she was right now and how she was teasing him with small grinds on his smooth head? He could even taste her, her lips moving over his, and he was loving every single minute of it.

She tasted so good and smelt so good too. Once she pulled her lips away from his, his lips latched onto the side of her neck, now kissing on her skin, wanting to please her. All he wanted to do was make her happy. Make her moan. Make her scream his name. Make her feel so much pleasure because of him.

"Uh Blaze, that feels so fuckin' good."

Blaze suddenly froze. That wasn't Anika's voice. That wasn't Anika's voice at all! His eyes suddenly shot up only to pull back away from the woman on his lap and to look up to see Candi smiling down at him.

"Why'd you stop?"

Blaze couldn't believe it. How was it, that in a matter of seconds of him dreaming of Anika, Candi had managed to sneak her way into his office and begin to seduce him? These chicks nowadays were way too fast and sly.

"If you don't feel like fuckin' here, we could go somewhere else... For the whole weekend," she suggested.

Blaze couldn't even respond. He was too shocked and confused right now. Why hadn't he stopped her? Why hadn't he even realized she had stepped into the room?

"I've got a new crib out of Atlanta that I go to when I need some time alone. You should come with me Blaze," she offered. "It's up in North Druid Hills."

North Druid Hills? Wasn't that the initials of Masika's...

Blaze never pushed a female off his body so quick. Hearing her words had him jumping straight out his chair, picking up his phone and running straight out the door.

He had finally worked out the meaning of Masika's text!

North Druid Hills.

CHAPTER 7 ~ FINDING HER

"A'ight, so North Druid Hills is located on the outskirts of Atlanta," Marquise informed the boys as they stood over the round wooden desk, all hands on the large map of Georgia they were looking at.

"And if he's got them somewhere there, we gotta start looking at dope spots and warehouses," Kareem explained.

"From what I've found out, The Bulls had one main dope spot up there," Marquise said, pointing to North Druid Hills. "But no one's been movin' weight up there for a few weeks now. I even tried contactin' the Bulls head. No one picked up."

"Well the newest rumor is," Kareem spoke up, "Lyons took over the territory and robbed the dope spot."

"So basically, Leek owns the area now?" Blaze asked his boys curiously.

"Exactly," Kareem stated in agreement. "If he owns the area now, he controls what goes in and out."

"And he can control who he decides to keep up there or not."

"So we all thinkin' the same shit right now, right?" Blaze queried, hoping he was right. "Leek's got Anika up there, right now."

Kareem and Marquise quickly nodded at their boy in agreement. They all felt and were thinking the same way. And they knew there was only one thing left to do right now.

"A'ight, let's go niggas."

***

Never had Blaze driven as fast as he was now. He couldn't stop. He wouldn't stop. Every single red light they had come across he had driven past. All he kept thinking of was the fact that his bae would be with him again. She would be back by his side, back in his bed, back as his main trap queen where she was supposed to be.

It was supposed to be a long drive up to North Druid Hills but because of Blaze's ferocious driving, it turned out to be much faster than usual. The only thing on Blaze's mind as he drove through the night, was reaching his woman.

Kareem and Marquise were especially glad that no cop managed to follow them or tag them along the way. They w lucky because if a cop car had pulled them over, they knew th would be in some serious trouble for the way he was driving. B ...ck it. They understood his determination. He just wanted to get to Anika.

When finally arriving at North Druid Hills, Kareem pulled up the location of the dope spot that was originally owned by The Bulls and ten minutes later, Blaze pulled nearby the warehouse.

They weren't sure what they were going to encounter when reaching the spot, but the boys were ready for anything. They were stocked up, each with their individual weapons, some hidden underneath their clothing and two guns in each of their hands.

Blaze held his red Russian AK-47 close by his side, while the other hand tightly gripped his silver .10mm ready to shoot any motherfucker that stood in his way of getting his lady back.

Slowly and slyly creeping round the sides of the warehouse, the boys decided to stay against the brick wall to run through their plan one more time.

"A'ight, so the buldin' has two entrances. The main one at the front, and the second one at the other side," Kareem explained quietly. "I'ma go through the back and try to break through if it's locked."

"And Blaze and I are goin' thru the fr-"

Blaze suddenly cut across Marquise, "Nah, go with 'Reem, Marq."

"What, why?" Kareem asked in a stern voice.

"I'm good on my own, I'on wan' you on yo' own though, 'Reem," Blaze responded seriously. "I'on want what happened to you, to happen ever again."

"It won't nigga," Kareem fumed. "I'm a grown ass nigga, I can handle me."

"Look, I know that, 'Reem, but just follow my orders right now," Blaze said firmly. "I'd prefer it if Marq was by yo' side."

"And what if somethin' was to hap-"

"We ain't got time for the couples' counseling session right now fools," Marquise quickly intervened. "We gotta get in and out, simple. I'll go with 'Reem. If niggas start shootin', niggas start shootin', and all

BAD FOR MY THUG 3: THE FINALE

we gotta do is shoot right back. We got this, just focus and stay on the job."

Kareem and Blaze nodded at Marquise with a determined facial expression before separating to the locations they had assigned themselves to.

Blaze crept round the front of the warehouse and noticed the closed large black door. Even though the spot appeared to be deserted, Blaze knew for a fact that it wasn't. It was almost as if he could feel her, sense her and hear her spiritually calling for him to save her. He just knew that it was now or never. He would rather it be now.

Blaze didn't care about all the risks he was taking to save his woman. A bunch of guys could literally jump out of nowhere and begin to shoot him down, but if he died knowing that he risked his life for Anika, he would die a content man.

Once making it to the front door, Blaze found himself suddenly kicking down the door violently and with only two kicks, he had managed to bust it wide open.

Inside the warehouse, all was dark and Blaze couldn't see a thing, or hear a thing either. That was until he suddenly heard a loud bang and a barrage of gunshots.

Just when he felt the need to run and take cover, the warehouse lights flicked on and a long silver corridor was revealed to him. On the other end of the corridor lay three men, now dead. And standing over the bodies was a proud Kareem and Marquise.

"Took care of these niggas already," Marquise loudly voiced. "No one else seems to be around. Leek and Jamal probably left for the night."

Not finding Leek and Jamal here wasn't really a surprise to Blaze. He figured that they were so confident in knowing that Blaze had no idea where they had his baby locked up, that they thought leaving the spot with only a few niggas to guard, would be okay. What fools they were.

Blaze didn't continue to a waste a single second not searching for Anika. The warehouse was only one floor and along the silver corridor that he stood at the start of, he could see four separate rooms. Frantically, he began to search in each one and it wasn't until he got to the final room, when he noticed the steel locked door.

Even as he tried kicking down the door, it was no use. It wouldn't budge, no matter how hard he tried to kick through; the shit just wasn't going to come down that easily. It only added to his current frustrations knowing that his bae was on the other side of the door. The door was the only thing that was stopping him from reaching the one person he wanted and needed right now.

"Yo' B', I got an idea," Kareem revealed. "I saw a steel bar near the back, lemme get it and we gon' use that to break it down."

Blaze didn't bother replying, he just nodded stiffly at Kareem and focused his attention on the locked door keeping him away from Anika.

Baby I'm comin'... I swear I'm just a few seconds away. I'm right here.

It was as if he could feel her connection to him and his thoughts, especially with him only being a few feet away from her.

When Kareem finally arrived with the steel bar, Blaze immediately took it from him and aimed straight into the middle of the door. After two hard knocks, the door was finally hit down and Blaze didn't waste any time bursting through the room.

The room was a medium sized room with nothing but concrete flooring and brick walls. In the corner of the room, Blaze immediately noticed Masika who appeared to be trying to sleep until she looked at who had just entered the room. Her eyes widened with surprise and happiness, but Blaze didn't bother paying any proper attention to her. If it wasn't for the fact that she was also being held against her own will, Blaze wouldn't have hesitated in sending a bullet right through her.

"Ma... Malik?"

Blaze's head immediately snapped in the direction of the gentle voice that he missed so much. Not hearing it for the past few weeks, still had him close to tears.

There she was, staring up at him with those pretty brown eyes of hers, that beautiful face of hers, still looking so innocent and fresh. She had Blaze filling up with an uncontrollable amount of happiness that resulted in tiny tears forming in his eyes.

"Anika," he gently called out to her, as he quickly sauntered close to where she was, and bent low to pull her into his arms. He planted a small kiss on her lips before speaking again. "Oh baby, I've missed you so much."

"Missed you too, Malik."

Within a few quick seconds, Anika was up and in his arms, Blaze leading her straight out of this hell to the rightful place where she belonged.

It was only when Blaze was halfway out the door with Anika securely in his arms, when Marquise asked about Masika.

Blaze had been so focused on Anika that he had completely forgotten about Masika. But nonetheless, she wasn't a traitor and if it wasn't for her message to Kareem, the boys probably wouldn't have even figured out where they were.

"Just leave the doors unlocked," Blaze loudly responded, knowing that Masika would hear his words. "She'll leave before the boys come and blow this shit all up."

The plan was to blow up the warehouse completely which would serve as a warning to Leek and especially Jamal, that this shit wasn't over. They had started something that Blaze knew he was going to have to finish. This was just the very start of the war.

The deadly war.

CHAPTER 8 ~ REUNITED

Having her sleep in his arms last night was amazing.

He wouldn't let her leave his sight. Even if she was going to the bathroom, going for a quick walk around the mansion, Blaze refused to leave her side.

The drive back home from the warehouse was silent, mostly due to the fact that Anika had fallen asleep in Blaze's arms. So there wasn't an opportunity for them to talk, but it didn't really bother Blaze about not talking. He was fine with looking down at his pretty lady as she slept peacefully, knowing that she had been saved.

Now, here she lay, still asleep on their California double king sized bed. Malik couldn't lie and say that he hadn't missed seeing her sleep on her side of the bed. When she wasn't around, the bed seemed empty and incomplete. He was tired of waking up in cold sweats, searching for her and realizing that she wasn't around.

However, now here she was and Blaze was going to make sure that it was his top priority that she stayed right where she belonged. With him.

All Blaze could do was continue to lay close to her and hold her in his arms. He paid attention to everything he could see and hear. The way her chest moved up and down as she breathed in and out, the light snores leaving her, and the way her gorgeous features looked when she was in a completely different head space.

Damn he had missed her.

Admiring her face, he noticed that she didn't seem to have any scars or bruises. Matter fact, she looked like she had been provided with daily washes and sanitary things. The clothes he had last seen her in, in Miami, were no longer on her. Instead, she was clothed in grey sweatpants that she hadn't seemed bother to remove yet.

He just thanked God that Leek or Jamal hadn't laid a single finger on her. He was already planning to add to the list of things he wanted to do to them by each scar on Anika, but with no scars meant that he had no reason to add to his already very long list.

It was only after ten minutes of staring at her, when she suddenly awoke, clearly startled by something.

Her eyes flashed open in a panic, thinking that she was in danger again but when Blaze's lips locked onto hers, Anika was reassured of her safety.

"Nika... You ain't gotta be scared no more," he whispered sweetly to her. "I got'chu baby."

She looked up into those mesmerizing grey eyes of his and found herself feeling much better knowing that she had been in his arms all night.

"Malik..."

"Yes bae?"

"I love you," she announced quietly.

It had been so long it seemed to Malik, since she had said those words to him. Her being away meant that he couldn't hear her say it often and he couldn't say it back. But now he could.

"I love you too," he responded, moving one of his hands onto her soft cheek. He gently began stroking her soft skin, trying to get her to relax. He wanted her as comfortable as possible and under no more stress at all, especially since he knew she was carrying his seed.

He wasn't sure when she wanted to discuss their baby, especially since she had just gotten back. But whenever she was ready to talk about it, he was down to listen. And he certainly wasn't going to rush his baby into things she wasn't ready for. He was taking things at her pace.

"How was yo' sleep?" he questioned her caringly.

"It was nice," she replied simply, looking down away from his heavy gaze. "Better than the sleeps I've been having before."

"And how you feelin' baby?"

She took a few seconds to respond, just remaining quiet to herself before looking directly at him, "I'm... I'm glad to be back with you Malik."

"And I'm so glad you back bae," he stated truthfully, moving closer to her. "I didn't know how long I was gon' cope without you by my side." He then began wrapping his arms around her, trying to be as close as he possibly could. "I'm so sorry for what happ-"

"Malik, it wasn't your fault. You couldn't have known that J-"

He cut her off. "Still baby, I apologize for that shit. I should have protected you as yo' fiancé, yo' man and yo' provider. It still kills me 'til this day that I wasn't able to make sure that you were safe. All that shit that went down could have been prevented if I had jus-"

Anika interrupted him with a quick kiss to his thick lips. She didn't want him blaming himself about the past anymore. She was back and she was safe with him now. He didn't need to be so hard on himself anymore.

It didn't take long for the subject of Leek and Jamal to pop up. While watching her eat her breakfast in bed, Blaze stayed by her side making sure she ate to get her strength up. She looked a bit lean and malnourished, and Blaze wasn't happy about it at all. So he cooked her a big breakfast and watched her eat. As she ate, she decided to speak about what had happened to her.

Blaze wasn't expecting her to be so open about what had gone on, but she seemed okay to talk about it.

From what she had said, they hadn't hurt her. Only Masika. They gave Anika fresh clothes, allowed her to wash, and food each day. But the food she hardly ate because it was horrible.

Blaze couldn't wait to get his hands on Leek and Jamal. He tried not to think about it too much but the more he tried the harder it became. He just knew that he was going to fuck them up individually, in the worst possible ways. And he was looking forward to it all very much.

After Anika's meal, she decided to have another nap. Blaze figured it was the pregnancy that was making her so tired, so he willingly let her sleep while he washed her plates in the kitchen downstairs.

While washing the plates, his doorbell suddenly rang. Hearing the loud, rapid sounds of the front bell had him confused and a little angry. He didn't want anyone disturbing his Queen as she slept.

"Yo chill, I'm comin'!"

When opening the door and seeing Sadie and Kareem, his anger quickly melted away. Sadie didn't waste a single second with her cousin. She pushed past him and quickly ran up his long white stairs leading to the second floor.

"Yo nigga," Blaze greeted 'Reem with a tight hug.

BAD FOR MY THUG 3: THE FINALE

"Yo, sorry about showin' up unannounced, when I told her 'bout Nika bein' back, she was already out the door."

"It's cool nigga," Blaze replied, understanding exactly why Sadie was so frantic to see Anika. Just the way he had missed his lady, her best friend and his cousin had missed her too.

Sadie ran across the corridor leading to Blaze's main bedroom and before she knew it, she had burst into his bedroom, only to see a peaceful Anika sleeping, that was until Sadie had burst into the room.

Anika's eyes fluttered open and she looked up to see who had entered the bedroom only to ask with surprise, "Sadie?"

"Anika!" Sadie exclaimed happily, running up to Anika's bedside.

Tears filled both their eyes and before they both knew it, they were tightly holding each other and crying.

"I was so worried," Sadie cried.

"Aww Sadie..."

"I thought they... I thought they had... done something bad to you, Nika," Sadie explained in between her sobs. "I was so scared and with 'Reem shot too, I didn't know what to do."

"I know hun," Anika whispered, rubbing on her back. "Everything's okay now though, I'm back now."

"Yes, you're back," Sadie said in a cheerier tone, breaking out their tight embrace. "I'm so happy and glad you're okay."

Anika smiled at her best friend happily, wiping her tears off her cheeks.

"And now that you're expecting, it's good you're back with Blaze."

Anika's happy smile immediately faded.

"Anika?" Sadie could sense Anika's shift in mood after her words. "What's wrong? Did I say something wrong?"

Anika kept silent, looking down at her hands joined with Sadie's.

"Anika talk to me. You're good right? The baby's fine?"

Anika could only keep silent again. Then she burst into tears.

"Anika," Sadie gently called out to her as she pulled her back into her arms. "Please tell me what's happened girl."

Anika continued to cry heavily, releasing all the sadness she had been feeling ever since she had been taken. She was trying to remain strong, especially for Blaze. She didn't want him to see her crying and start worrying about her like he always did.

But now she couldn't hold it all in anymore.

"Anika, please talk to me. I'm your best friend. You can tell me anything."

Anika took a deep breath before making her dreaded announcement.

"I lost the baby."

CHAPTER 9 ~ RELEVATIONS

"How did you find out?" Sadie gently asked, rubbing Anika's back as she lay her head on her chest.

"The fourth day I was there," Anika slowly began. "I went to the bathroom and I just remember seeing blood. And not just the usual amount I have when I'm on my period or anything. An unusual amount of blood."

"I'm so sorry sweetheart," Sadie said, trying to bring some comfort to her best friend. "You're still young though. You and Blaze have plenty of time to start your family."

"I know Sadie but I was really looking forward to having his child now," Anika explained. "I wanted us to start now, especially since he proposed to me."

"You still have time though darling, so don't think it's the end of the world."

"Yeah, I guess you're right... But I can't stop thinking about it."

"Have you told Blaze yet?" Sadie queried curiously.

"Not yet," Anika responded sadly. "And I'm dreading telling him."

Anika wasn't sure exactly how she was going to tell Malik about losing their baby and she didn't want him to start beating himself up about it. But unfortunately for Anika, Malik had already found out.

"I'm sorry man... Y'all still got time to make plenty of babies though," Kareem informed Blaze, watching as he stood in the corner of his modern styled kitchen, staring into space. It was as if he was in a completely different realm right now.

After greeting Kareem at the door, they both decided to go up and check on how their girls were settling together after not seeing each other for some time. But when they got to the closed door of the bedroom, Blaze immediately heard Sadie asking Anika to tell her what was wrong.

Blaze then put a hand to Kareem's chest, stopping him from trying to enter the room. They both stood and listened to Anika tell Sadie what was wrong.

"I lost the baby."

Blaze felt like a million pieces of glass had been suddenly shoved into his heart. He immediately turned on his heels away from the room, headed downstairs to the kitchen, with a worried Kareem following.

Now here he stood, thinking about what could have been.

He couldn't lie and say he wasn't excited to be a father because he was. He had been so excited that he had already began to think of colors for one of the spare guest bedrooms upstairs, that would have been the baby's nursery.

Now hearing that Anika had lost his baby, their baby, felt horrible.

If only he had protected her better. If only he had come back from his meeting with Sergio quicker. If only he had been smarter. None of this shit would have happened.

"Blaze?"

Blaze looked up at his best friend staring at him worriedly.

"You gon' be good nigga. Don't worry. Things happen sometimes, but we just gotta learn from them and keep movin'."

Blaze nodded stiffly before staring back into the space around him. Even as hard as he was trying to fight back the tears trying to form in his eyes, he couldn't. And before he knew it, tiny tears were leaving his eyes.

Kareem quickly sauntered close to his brother and embraced him into his arms. He didn't like seeing his boy like this, but he was always going to be there to comfort him, no matter what.

"I promise you things gon' be alright, bro. You and Anika gon' have all the babies you want soon and you'll be happier than ever before, I promise you bro."

Blaze continued to cry and nod while staying in his brother's arms. He appreciated the comfort and the love. It was the only thing that was motivating him to stay positive right now.

***

"I'm sorry I didn't tell you earlier Malik, I was just so scared you know... I didn't know how to really come out and tell you that I had lost the baby."

"I understand," Blaze responded simply, looking into Anika's pretty brown eyes as she spoke. "It's not yo' fault, baby. Shit happens."

"We didn't even really get a chance to talk about it. The day I found out was the day I got... taken."

"I know, bae."

"I'm sorry I lost the baby," she apologized sadly. "I know you're probably blaming me and thinking I should have been more careful and I should have told you so-"

"Hey," Blaze lifted her hand so he could hold it in his own. "It's not yo' fault Anika. Let's just use this as a lesson, and a chance for us to focus on the future. We got plenty of time to make all the babies we want and need. A'ight? I love you, I'm your man. I ain't neva gon' blame you for shit that ain't yo' fault. Okay?"

Anika nodded at him with a weak smile.

"Now come here and give yo' man some sugar," Blaze seductively ordered her. "You know he's missed you so much."

Anika's weak smile immediately began to grow stronger and she got up out her seat and obeyed his orders. She went to sit on his lap and let him wrap his arms around her before gently kissing his lips.

It was still too early for Anika to make love again. As much as she wanted to be with Blaze again, feel his touch and feel him inside her... She was scared and quite nervous. She knew that within a few days though, she would probably be feeling up to it. But right now she was absolutely fine with just kissing.

***

"You feelin' alright babe? I know you were a bit upset about Anika," Kareem voiced gently to Sadie as he held her close to his body while they lay on the couch together.

"I'm better than before, that's for sure," Sadie responded with a soft sigh. "I felt so bad for her you know... I know how bad she wants kids of her own."

"Same with Blaze," Kareem stated. "But hey, they got all the time in the world to make as many babies as they want. And so do we." His dipped his head to the side of her neck, only to sniff in her seductive scent and begin to kiss on her soft skin. "We could even start now if you want."

"'Reem... Not right now, I'm tired."

"We just got back though," Kareem protested. "Why exactly are you tired baby?"

"I don't know," she explained quietly. "I'd rather just eat somethin' and then rest. Then maybe after all that... We can do whatever you wanna do."

"Whateva I wanna do?" he questioned her curiously with a sexy smirk.

Sadie couldn't help but chuckle lightly at him, knowing that due to his freakish ways, he was already beginning to think of all the freaky things they could do together. "I forgot how much of a freak you are 'Reem."

"And that's one of the many reasons why you love me," he said, softly pecking her neck before adding, "I don't know why you tryna play like you ain't a freak too. Wit' yo' sexy, freaky ass..."

"And that's one of the many reasons why you love me," Sadie announced smartly.

"You got that right," Kareem concluded before lifting her chin up, so he could easily lock his lips onto hers so they could kiss each other.

Their tongues began to dance passionately and lips moved together in a way that was so sweet, loving, but filled with a heated lust.

Sadie soon felt Kareem's hands moving up her waist, up her stomach and before she knew it, both his hands were cupping both of her breasts. A strong fire of desire began to light within her, but she knew that she wasn't ready to make love right now. She would rather get her energy up with some much needed food, and use it all up after.

"Hmm... 'Reem, not right now," Sadie ordered, pulling her lips away from his. "I'm hungry and I'm tired."

"But babe, you got a nigga feenin' for yo' ass right now," he said with a light groan. "Just let me get some now. You can eat after."

"But I'd rather eat now and get my energy up so I can be ready to do whatever you wanna do."

"But ba-"

BAD FOR MY THUG 3: THE FINALE

"Whatever you wanna do 'Reem," Sadie concluded happily before shifting away from Kareem, so she could get up and head to his kitchen.

"Whateva I wanna do?" Kareem queried, biting his lips as he watched her get up.

She turned around to face him and nodded with a sexy wink before walking away from him.

All Kareem could do was smile with excitement, knowing that Sadie was willing to bend over backwards tonight for him in bed.

And he meant that literally.

Ding!

The sudden vibration from his iPhone diverted his attention from thinking about his baby, and he pulled out his phone's current text notification.

Kareem looked down at his bright screen with curiosity and slight annoyance. Slight annoyance that this chick was still in his life.

"I'm ready to meet up and discuss what you wanted."

The quicker he got Satin out his life, the better. He wanted Sadie to be his wife and in order for that to happen successfully, he needed to no longer be married.

Kareem: *"Alright, I'll let u know when to come."*

Satin: *"Do u already have the papers drawn up?"*

Kareem: *"Yea'"*

Satin: *"Wow you're fast."*

Kareem: *"Got to be."*

Satin: *"Why?"*

Kareem: *"U already know why Satin."*

Satin: *"No I don't."*

Satin: *"I don't understand why u don't want to give us a chance anymore."*

Satin: *"Don't u want me?"*

Kareem: *"I don't feel that way about u anymore Satin."*

Satin: *"But I love u K."*

Kareem: *"U don't."*

Kareem: *"U just pissed I'm with someone else."*

Kareem: *"And that someone else ain't u."*

Satin: *"I want us to get back together K."*

Satin: *"I don't want a divorce. I never did. That's not why I came here to see u."*

Kareem: *"That's why I called u. I'm with someone else. Happy."*

Satin: *"Do you love her?"*

Kareem: *"Yes, I do."*

Satin: *"U sure?"*

Kareem: *"Positive."*

Satin: *"I don't believe u."*

Kareem: *"Why not?"*

Satin: *"U couldn't say it to my face."*

Kareem: *"I ain't wanna hurt yo' feelings."*

Satin: *"Liar. U just don't love her. She ain't like me."*

Satin: *"I bet she don't treat you like I did."*

Kareem: *"You right."*

Satin: *"I bet she don't fuck you like I did."*

Kareem: *"You right."*

Satin: *"I bet she don't kiss you like I did."*

Kareem: *"U right. You know why you right?"*

Satin: *"Why baby?"*

Kareem: *"Cuz she treats me better than you did. She don't fuck around with other niggas behind my back. She fucks me better than u ever could. I ain't even gotta pretend to like eating her out, I do that shit every day because it makes me happy. It keeps me fed too. And her shit definitely don't stink like yours did. She definitely don't kiss like you did. Yo' kisses were shit, you ain't even know what you were doing. But Sadie? Her kisses make my dick hard even with just one simple move. So you right, she ain't like you. She BETTER."*

Satin: *"I hate u."*

Kareem: *"I know."*

Kareem: *"I'ma let you know when to come sign the papers too."*

Kareem: *"Have a great day. I know I will. With my future wife."*

And after getting no responses from her anymore, all Kareem could do was sigh with relief at the fact that Satin had finally gotten the message.

He was done with her.

CHAPTER 10 ~ SLY CHICKS

"Aww, thank you baby, I appreciate you making me breakfast."

"It's alright, you know I gotta make sure my baby goes to work on a full stomach," Kareem stated lovingly as he began to dish Sadie's food out for her. "Looking forward to yo' big job today?"

"Yeah, I am really," she responded. "I'm doing a whole bridal train today and I'm so excited about doing the bride's makeup and nails. But I'm nervous, too."

Being a MUA and a nail technician, definitely had it perks for Sadie. She loved that she could have lots of free time to work on building her brand, days off, and then be called for a job ready to provide her wonderful services.

"You gon' do an amazin' job today baby," Kareem told her confidently. "You great at what you do, so don't you eva be scared. You talented and yo' hard work always shows."

"Thank you, baby," Sadie thanked him, feeling quite gassed at his lovely compliments. She got up out her seat and went to where he was standing cooking, and wrapped her arms tightly around his muscular physique. "I love you."

"Love you too, freaky girl," he responded, turning around so that he could turn to kiss her.

After eating breakfast, Sadie was quickly began gathering her tools needed to do the makeup and nails of her clients today. Kareem helped her collect her equipment and place it in her car.

Then before he knew it, they were done, she was kissing him goodbye, and he was sitting on his couch staring down at his bright phone screen.

"I'll be there around 3?"

Satin was coming over today to Kareem's apartment, to finally sign the divorce papers that would free him from her clutches forever.

Kareem: *"Cool."*

After replying to her text, in came a notification from his squad group chat with his boys.

Marquise: "No word on Leek or Jamal yet."

Blaze: "Boys still searchin' right?"

Marquise: "Yup."

Kareem: "It's been a week since we got Nika back. They gon' come lookin' soon."

Marquise: "And we gon' get their asses."

Kareem: "How Anika settling in B'?"

Blaze: "She a'ight... Just been sleepin' mostly."

Marquise: "In yo' arms I bet."

Blaze: "Yeah nigga, where else?"

Kareem: "A'ight lover boy so when you down for leavin' her home alone?"

Blaze: "I ain't sure... I ain't really thought 'bout it yet."

Marquise: "You can't be scared forever B'."

Blaze: "I know, I know... I ain't really that scared."

Kareem: "But you still scared."

Marquise: "Just get some boys watchin' the house or somethin'. She'll be good."

Blaze: "That don't sound like a bad idea. Yeah I think I might do that nigga."

Kareem: "Do that. You gotta be okay with leavin' her by herself sometimes. There's no way those fools will try takin' her again. Especially not in yo' own home."

Marquise: "I agree. Get some of the boys securing yo' crib and you straight."

Blaze: "Yeah, I'ma do it. Thanks for the idea 'Reem."

Kareem: "You welcome."

Marquise: "Talk to y'all later, Naomi trippin' right now."

Blaze: "Cool."

Kareem: "See ya."

***

"Blaze stopppp!" Anika exclaimed, giggling as Blaze began tickling her while she lay on the center of their California bed. "Malik! Stoppp!"

Ever since Blaze had found out that tickling was one of her weaknesses, a few months back and he had always been using it to his advantage to get Anika to cheer up. She seemed a bit down before but now that he had started, she couldn't control the laughter or smiles forming from her mouth.

"I know how much you love me ticklin' you and shit," he chuckled, as he continued to tickle her, knowing full well that she didn't like being tickled one bit.

It made her laugh so much, and would sometimes give her hiccups when she was younger. She tried to stop him by grabbing his arms, but Blaze was bigger, stronger, and much faster than her. There was no way that it was going to work.

"Malik!" she continued to giggle, unable to control herself.

"Do you wan' me to stop baby?" he questioned her amusingly, still using his hands to tickle various spots around her body. He took a glimpse at her flashy engagement ring on her left hand, and he couldn't help but light up with happiness knowing that they were soon going to get married. They hadn't started planning yet, but Blaze knew it was only a matter of time before Anika got busy preparing. How big or small she wanted it, she could have it. Money wasn't an object.

"Yasssssssss... Malik..." She couldn't stop giggling and it was starting to hurt her stomach. "Pleaseee!"

He finally stopped and this gave her the opportunity to breathe and catch some well needed air. "Feelin' betta now?"

She took one look at his cheeky grin and gave him a fake frown before grinning back at him. "Much better."

Blaze bent low to her lips, pecking them gently before moving away to stand up straight. He said nothing as he turned on his heels towards their en-suite bathroom.

Anika wondered why he had just decided to up and leave her without trying to pursue the subject of sex yet. It had been a week since she had been back and he still hadn't tried to get some. She couldn't lie and say that she didn't appreciate his patience and consideration, but right now she was feenin' for him. Especially now that she had been to the doctor's for a checkup and been assured that losing her baby wasn't going to cause any future complications.

BAD FOR MY THUG 3: THE FINALE

All she could think about every time she took one glimpse at that sexy body of his, was that she wanted to jump him and make a new baby.

"Baby!"

His sudden call from the bathroom had her alert and ready.

"Yes Malik?"

"You ready?" he asked.

"For what babe?"

"For yo' bath," he explained simply.

"Yeah..." She sighed softly before getting up out of bed and heading to their bathroom.

"Hurry up, I don't wan' it to get cold, ma." Blaze said to her, as he sat by the warm bubble bath that he had made for her.

He just wanted to treat his woman tonight. He knew how down she had been ever since the whole kidnapping incident, and she was only just getting used to being back. Malik wanted to make Anika feel good, physically, emotionally and mentally.

He wasn't going to try and force having sex with her right now, especially since he didn't think that she was ready for it. He hadn't had her in almost a month now and he knew that when he did, he was probably going to almost break the girl's damn legs. So right now, being patient was the motive.

Blaze had lit lavender scented candles all around the bathroom, and neatly scattered red and pink rose petals on the marble floor. A bottle of Anika's favorite champagne and fresh chocolate covered strawberries, were sitting close by the bath. There was also a small wooden stool where he could sit next to the bathtub and wash his beautiful Queen, massage her, and just watch her take a bath. In the background, Trey Songz's "Massage" played, setting the romantic mood.

Once she stepped into the bathroom, the excitement in her pretty eyes was undeniable. And Malik was just happy to know that she was happy.

"Malik... All this for me?" He stood up and walked towards her.

"Yes sweetheart, just for you." He slowly reached down to her grey sweats and began pulling them down for her, pushing them down her body and letting them fall to the ground.

Seeing those bare, long, sexy legs of hers was enough to make him quickly grow in his pants. But he knew that he had to remain patient.

"Thank you, I love you," she smiled at him, leaning closer to his lips.

"I love you too," he told her before pressing his lips onto hers. The kiss was quick, sweet and addictive. He could stand there and kiss her all day, but right now he had a treat for her that he wanted to complete.

He pulled away from her lips, turning away from her only to go and sit on the wooden stool.

"Strip the rest of yo' clothes off and... come in babe."

Blaze watched as she obeyed his orders and took off her remaining clothes before making her way closer to the white tub. She stepped into the bubbles and began settling in.

Blaze had sure missed seeing his baby naked. Every single part of her body had been sculpted to perfection, and naked? She looked even sexier and tempting than she did when she was clothed. He knew he was so blessed to have an amazing, gorgeous woman in his life.

"*Mmm...* Feels so nice and warm," she commented, getting comfortable and relaxing her back.

"That's good." He licked his lips seductively at her, as he reached for her bottle of champagne and got her a glass.

"Baby, why don't you come in with me?" Anika questioned him, slowly starting to wash herself.

Her question had definitely taken him by surprise. He didn't think she would want him in with her. "Nah, I want to be the one watchin' yo' pretty ass take a bath and makin' sure that you leave this bath feelin' good," he informed her sweetly, moving closer to her and bringing her glass of champagne to her lips.

Anika drank it slowly, trying to savor the sweet taste. She loved the romantic side of Blaze. That was definitely a trait of his that she had missed. She had been the only one able to see this side of him.

BAD FOR MY THUG 3: THE FINALE

After she had had a small sip, Blaze reached for the chocolate covered strawberries.

"Ooo baby, chocolate strawberries... My fav," she squealed with delight. He knew how much she liked them.

He began to feed her one, watching as she licked the chocolate head slowly, before eating it. He noticed how she stared directly at him as she licked the smooth head of the berry, immediately making him think of another place she could lick the smooth head of. However, he quickly shook the dirty thought out of his head.

"You like how it tastes, baby?" Blaze asked her, getting off his stool and deciding to kneel on the bathroom floor so he could be as close to her as possible. She nodded, biting her luscious lips sexily.

His knees were on the floor and his arms were resting on the tub's edge. He had a good view of her right now. Actually no - scratch that - He had an amazing view of her right now.

Even though the bubble bath was covering the main parts of her body, Blaze could still use his hands to push them out the way and admire his beautiful fiancée.

And that's exactly what he did.

Malik kept his eyes on hers as he lowered his hand into her warm bath. Gently, he touched her left breast and noticed how pleased she looked as he began to massage it. He decided to use his free left hand to massage her other breast, so he could please both.

Anika deeply sighed, closing her eyes and enjoying the feel of his hands touching her breasts. She was glad that he was finally considering them making love, because she knew how much she would be craving him after this bubble bath.

"Blaze..." She whispered his name, her eyes still shut. "I love you touching me... So much." Of course she loved her thug touching her. He knew all the right places to touch. All the right ways to touch her and leave her wanting more.

His hands left her breasts and slowly trailed down her flat stomach and in between her juicy thighs. He wanted to be patient but it seemed like she wanted him to forget all about being patient. From the way she had been looking at him and now talking, it was clear that she wanted him as much as he wanted her.

"Shit Blaze," she softly whimpered, as his wet fingers began to massage her clit underneath the warm bath water.

"Relax, baby. I'm just here to make you feel good." His long fingers started massaging her clit faster and faster.

The faster he got, the louder Anika's sweet moans were. He knew how insane he was driving her and he was loving every single second of it. Once he pushed two fingers into her and kept pushing them in and out of her tight pussy, her sexy moans were uncontrollable.

"Blaze! Oh God... Yesss! Uhh..." Blaze had always found his baby's moans sexy. She didn't moan too awfully loud or too quiet. She moaned just right and it always turned him on.

"Don't stop... Agh! Malik..."

He slowly released his fingers from her, only to bring them out the lukewarm water, straight to his lips. He licked her juices off his fingers, staring directly at her and watched the surprised, but turned on facial expression on her face.

"Baby, I need you to get in with me... Please?" she tried to plead with him, but his treat for her wasn't over yet. And he certainly didn't want to rush things.

"No Nika... I ain't done yet. Just let me do my job by makin' you feel good." He grinned at her, revealing his pearly whites. "You know I don't wanna rush you baby. We ain't gotta have se-"

"I want you though, Malik," she revealed. "I miss you and I want to feel you inside me. Right now Malik."

That did it for Malik.

Five minutes later, he had finished washing all over her body and decided to give into what she said she wanted.

Him.

"Fuck... Nika, baby."

Anika's body tensed as she slowly slipped his dick inside her pussy. Blaze swore he saw stars as he felt her tight walls clenching around his dick. He had missed feeling her so much.

She was sitting frontwards on Blaze's lap, completely naked and wet. She was in control. Whatever she wanted to do, he was down for it. She was his woman and however she wanted their sex to go today, that's the way things were going to go.

BAD FOR MY THUG 3: THE FINALE

She had her hands tightly holding on to his muscular shoulders, and her lustful eyes locked onto his. Feeling his big, long length after all these days, had her currently feeling an indescribable high that she knew she didn't want to come down from.

Blaze had his hands placed on her small waist and watched her as she began to ride him up and down.

Their foreheads pressed together and Anika flicked her tongue over his bottom lip, pressing their mouths together in a heated kiss. She captured his tongue with hers and sucked gently on it. Then she pulled back from the wet kiss before speaking. "I missed you... so much Malik."

She continued to ride him up and down, increasing the speeds of her moves, only adding to Blaze's pleasure.

He groaned lightly before responding, "I missed you so much too, girl."

"I love you Mr. King."

He stared deeply into her lust filled eyes and knowing that this was the woman he was going to spend the rest of his life with before replying, "I love you too, Mrs. King."

***

Kareem watched as Satin grabbed the black pen and slowly reached for the white paper laid out in front of her. He noticed the way she began to pretend to read the document, like she really thought she was getting a dime from him.

"Don't read it Satin, just sign it," he ordered firmly.

She suddenly looked up at him. "But I want to know what I'm getti-"

"You ain't gettin' shit," he retorted. "Just sign it."

Satin obeyed, pressing the pen down to the paper so that she could sign. Once she had signed, Kareem sighed deeply. He was finally free to marry the real woman he wanted.

"I wish you nothin' but the best Satin and I kn... Woah! Satin, chill," Kareem suddenly protested, trying to push her away as she came closer to him and tried to kiss him.

"What, no goodbye kiss?" she asked with a perfectly arched brow.

"No Satin," he snapped. "You know I'm with Sadie. Stop fuckin' playin'."

"I don't see nothin' wrong with a goodbye kiss," she cooed sweetly and began moving her hands up her black trench coat.

Kareem thought that it was a little odd that she had walked up to his apartment with such a long coat, but he said nothing about it. All he cared about was her signing the divorce papers. However, seeing her now unbuttoning her coat had him a little worried.

And he had every right to be.

Because as soon as she unbuttoned her coat, she pushed it off her shoulders and let it fall to the floor.

Satin was dressed in nothing but black lingerie. And not just any type of lingerie. It was the type that a female wore for her man. The sexy kind of lingerie that told him you wanted to get fucked as soon as possible.

"Satin, you need to go."

She didn't listen though. She only began to saunter closer to him and with each step she took closer, Kareem took a step back. It wasn't until he was backed up against his living room wall that Satin jumped on him.

"Satin, no, I don't wan... Sa... Sati..." His words kept getting cut off because of Satin's forceful lips sealing on his.

While forcefully kissing him, Satin grabbed both of his hands and moved them to her ass. When he tried to move his hands away, Satin kept her tight and hard grip on his hands, stopping him from trying to move them.

"Satin, get the fu...Sto...Sa..." Each word continued to get cut off and Kareem found her lips moving overs his, overpowering his words. It shouldn't have been that hard to get Satin off him, but for some reason it was.

And before Kareem knew it, he was kissing her back like old times, remembering the sweet memories they used to have with each other, all those years ago. Satin had managed to seduce him, with just one quick act.

Through all the sweet memories flooding back into his mind and passionately kissing her, Kareem didn't hear the key turn in his lock. And he definitely didn't hear the slow opening of the front door.

But he definitely heard the throwing of a large vase across the room, hitting the wall of where Kareem stood.

His mind immediately became alert and all happy thoughts of Satin went flying out the window. He violently pushed her off his body and looked straight ahead only to see an angry Sadie now removing her earrings and her shoes.

"Sadie, I swear I can explain!" he shouted, terrified and guilty.

Sadie turned to face him and stared at him and Satin with a neutral facial expression, only adding to his fears each second. Then she spoke up.

"I'ma fuck you up and your bitch," she announced with a devilish smile.

Then she charged straight at them both.

CHAPTER 11 ~ BROKEN TRUST

All Sadie could see was red.

When she entered Kareem's apartment, all she could think of was quickly picking up her eye shadow kit and heading back to the bridal party awaiting her amazing skills. She had been so embarrassed at the fact that she had forgotten one of the most important elements of making up her clients' faces. So all that was on her mind as she drove back home to 'Reem's was getting her eye shadow kit and heading straight back.

But this right here took the icing off the cake. This right here took her from her happy place, to her angry place, filled with nothing but negativity and destruction.

Seeing the way the man who claimed he loved her so much, kissed his ex-wife and hold onto her so sexually, had Sadie fuming.

"Sadie, I swear it's not what it loo-"

"Shut the hell up!" Sadie shouted angrily, cutting him off as she grabbed onto Satin, who seemed to be trying to make a run for it.

"Sadie, please!"

Sadie decided on wasting no time in trying to hear what Kareem had to say, or respond to whatever he thought was going to save him or help the situation. Nothing was going to save the current situation. There would be no reconciliation.

Only ass whoopings.

Kareem observed fearfully as Sadie grabbed onto Satin's long, straightened weave and pulled her closer towards her.

All he saw next was Sadie's fists hitting and pounding any and every angle of Satin's face. He knew his baby could fight, but actually seeing her in one had never happened. Until now. And he couldn't lie... Seeing his baby hold her ground, had him slightly getting turned on.

He could hear Satin screaming, trying to fight back, and calling for Kareem to save her, but he knew that if he tried to get involved Sadie would be coming for him at all angles. So he stayed in his place, and continued to watch a determined Sadie beat the shit out of Satin.

BAD FOR MY THUG 3: THE FINALE

Every hit, every pound, every pull, only enticed Sadie to keep on going on. She had a point to prove here and she needed Satin to understand it as clear as possible. *You make a move on my man, you get your ass beat.*

Once satisfied with all her hits, pounds and fully content knowing that Satin had learned her lesson, she dragged the bitch across the floor by pulling on her hair, and flung her straight out the door. Satin landed face first on the hard floor outside and Sadie couldn't help but smile at how things had turned out now. Sadie also made sure she picked up the trench coat that Satin had rocked up here in, and threw it out right along with her.

"Don't you ever bring your dumb ass 'round here again, you stupid ass bitch," Sadie spat before slamming the door violently. She took a deep breath before trying to remain calm, but it was no use.

The tears immediately burst through and all Sadie could think was, *what if?*

What if she hadn't come back home to get the rest of her make-up equipment? What if she hadn't burst in? What if Kareem never stopped kissing Satin? What if they had ended up having sex, right there in his living room, and what if she never said a fucking word?!

Sadie's mind continued to race with what ifs and the tears kept seeping through, only adding to the pain in her broken heart.

She shut her eyes tightly to try and stop the tears, but it didn't do anything. The tears were still managing to escape and make their way past her eyelids.

She was completely heartbroken and she knew it too.

"Baby I'm so so-"

"Don't fucking touch me," she snapped with fury, pushing him away from her as he tried to make a move to wrap his arms around her. "Don't fucking touch me 'Reem! I should kill you right now! I should fucking kill you!"

Kareem still ignored her and continued making an effort to touch her. "Sadie, I know shit looks bad but I didn't wa-"

Sadie pushed him against the beige wall and grabbed onto his neck in an attempt to strangle him. She was sick of hearing him trying to plead his case when he had been caught.

"I still found you kissing the bitch," she retorted, tightening her grip on his neck. "I don't care what you have to say! You still cheated, regardless of what she tried to do."

"Sa... Sa.. die... I'm... c-chokin'," Kareem choked out in a distressed and painful voice.

She knew she was hurting him, but she didn't care. He needed to suffer as much as she had when she saw him against the wall, holding Satin's ass and kissing her back.

Niggas thought that it was cool to creep around with the next bitch and think that their main bitch wasn't going to do anything about it. Well, Sadie knew she was definitely going to do something about it.

"We're over, fool!" she concluded before releasing her grip around Kareem's neck and walking off towards his bedroom. It was time for her to pack her shit up and get the fuck out.

Kareem breathed deeply, moving his hand around his neck, trying to soothe the pain of Sadie's hard grip around it.

The woman he loved, really was crazy. And if she meant that she wanted to kill him, then she was serious.

But they couldn't be over! Kareem wouldn't allow it.

Over his dead body was he letting her crazy ass leave him.

***

"Baby, I want you to promise me one thing..."

Blaze looked down at his lady, laying her head happily on his bare chest and gently stroking it.

"Anythin' bae," he promised automatically, without even knowing what she wanted.

"Malik, you haven't even heard what the promise is yet," Anika said with a light giggle, lifting her head off his chest and siting up straight.

"I'on care," he said simply. "There's nothin' I wouldn't do for you baby."

He just loved the way they had been chilling naked in bed together, making love, and were now cuddled up under the soft, silk, violet sheets.

"So you promise to do whatever I ask?" she queried suspiciously.

He nodded, trying to reassure her.

"I want you to promise me Malik, that you won't kill Jamal."

Blaze immediately burst into laughter, staring at Anika as she stared at him. He expected her to laugh with him, indicating to him that she was joking, but when the serious expression on her pretty face remained, he knew it wasn't a joke.

"What? Nika, you can't be ser-"

"You promised, Malik," she stated seriously. "You said there's nothing you wouldn't do for me. I don't want you to have any more blood on your hands. Jamal isn't worth it."

"But Nika, I can't not get them ba-"

She cut him off again. "You promised, Malik."

"Yo, what I tell yo' ass 'bout cuttin' me off," he retorted.

"And I'm gonna keep cutting you off until you confirm your promise, Malik," she announced boldly.

He told himself that he would never want to upset his baby ever again after the whole Masika and Desiree incident. His heart was hers and whatever she needed, he had it for her. There was nothing he wouldn't do for her.

So he had to confirm his promise.

Now thinking about it, he didn't know what he was supposed to do. If he wasn't going to kill Jamal, what was the point in looking for the guy?

He could always kill Leek, but even then he knew Anika would find out and she wouldn't be happy.

So what was the point of it all?

Even though he couldn't kill Jamal, he could still beat the shit out of him and teach him a lesson. But Blaze knew that doing that wouldn't make him satisfied.

From looking for Jamal and Leek, and looking after Anika and making sure she was happy 24/7, Blaze couldn't lie and say he wasn't stressed. Because he was.

To top it all off, Sergio had been requesting to see him soon to discuss the matter of Blaze becoming his own connect.

MISS JENESEQUA

A couple of months ago, Blaze never would have questioned the subject. He straight away would have been all in for it. But now, he had Anika to think about. She was basically his life now and he knew that if he was to become the connect, that would affect things in their relationship.

He would always be busy, working and probably only see her in the mornings and a couple nights a week. He wouldn't want things to become distant between them and he certainly wouldn't be comfortable with leaving her all by herself, even though he had security watching the house 24/7 now.

Becoming the connect would mean that things would be ten times harder and trying to leave the game as soon as Anika wanted him to, would be almost impossible.

He had too much to consider, and not enough time. A decision had to be made very soon and whatever it was, Blaze would have to be ready to face it.

***

She knew that sending one text would get her into trouble.

She knew that she would have been caught eventually.

She knew that she would suffer.

But she still did it.

And for who?

The only man she had ever loved and truly cherished. The man she regretted creeping out on and lying to.

Only to be left behind and forgotten.

"You idiot! You ruined everythin'!"

Looking into the deadly eyes of the man she had had one kid with and seeing how determined he was to kill her as he tightened his grip around her neck, had Masika no longer scared. At least now she would be free.

No more hiding.

No more running.

No more lies.

She would be free.

BAD FOR MY THUG 3: THE FINALE

The only person she would miss would be Blaze. She just hoped that one day he would remember how much she truly felt about him and all she was willing to do for him. She just hoped he remembered the days she was down to be the Bonnie to his Clyde, whenever he wanted.

Masika felt the air in her lungs getting tighter and tighter by the second, and she knew it was only a matter of minutes before she would be gone.

And she didn't care. She would rather be free than face all the pain, humiliation and sadness she had been through these past few months.

Leek watched with great satisfaction at Masika's non-struggling behavior. He found it odd at first that she wasn't fighting back, but then he quickly didn't care.

It was her fault that Anika had managed to escape free with Blaze's help. And it was her fault that Blaze and his crew had managed to easily blow up their main warehouse.

So now he had to follow Jamal's orders.

"Get rid of her."

She had to be punished for being a snake, a liar and a hoe. Leek would never forgive her for sneaking around with him and still being with Blaze at the same time. Once upon a time he loved her, that's the only reason why he agreed to have a kid with her. But now he was left with no kid, and defeated at knowing that Anika was safe and sound.

The light had finally left Masika's eyes, and she was no longer breathing desperately against Leek's tight hands.

She had paid for being a traitor and a snake.

And next to pay was Blaze and his entire stupid squad. They had to die. It was the only way that things could be sorted and the score would be settled. They had to die.

Leek would make sure of it.

CHAPTER 12 ~ SERIOUS TALKS

"The bitch seduced me! And I was tryna explain that shit to Sadie, but she won't even listen to me. Every time I tried to speak, she threatened to kill me and she's crazy so I ain't tryna risk dyin'."

"So you let her go?" Marquise queried with a silly smirk.

"After she strangled a nigga, of course I fuckin' let her go! I told y'all I ain't tryna risk dyin' yet. I gotta get her back first man..."

"Well you did fuck up," Blaze began in a firm tone. "After I told yo' dumb ass not to fuck up again, 'Reem."

Kareem sighed deeply before responding, "I know B', but it ain't my fault, I swear!"

"You let Satin into yo' crib, right?" Blaze questioned him through hooded eyes.

"Yeah bu-"

"And you let her kiss you first right?"

"Yeah... But it wasn't m-"

"So how is this shit not yo' fault, fool?" Blaze asked rudely.

"It ain't! I swear I ain't even want her to come over, but how was I 'posed to get her to quickly sign the papers wit'out bailin' out on me. I had to make her feel comfortable and it worked, because before she tried that dumb shit wit' me, she signed the papers."

"Well at least you got one good thing out of this whole situation nigga," Marquise commented with a hearty chuckle.

"Yeah, I guess so," Kareem stated with a shrug. "Man, I just gotta get her back... She keeps on ignoring my calls, won't even reply to my texts, like what a nigga gotta do to get her to listen to me?"

"Stop fuckin' up," Blaze retorted. "Then she won't call things off between you two."

"Hey, like I said, it wasn't entirely my fault. I know I made some dumb mistakes lately with Satin, but I swear all that shit is out the window. She signed the papers, so now I gotta focus on Sadie."

"You do that," Blaze replied sternly. "Or else the next time you fuck up... It won't be Sadie killin' yo' ass."

Kareem could understand why Blaze was so over protective when it came to Sadie. She was his cousin and even though they weren't cousins by blood, she still meant a lot to him. She was basically a sister to him, so seeing him pissed at her being upset wasn't a surprise.

"I promise no more fuckin' up, I'ma make it up to her B'. I promise."

"So what's the word on Jamal and Leek?" Blaze asked the boys curiously. He had hardly been thinking about Jamal and Leek lately, especially since he had been so busy with making Anika good. And ever since he promised not to kill Jamal, the anxiousness to find him wasn't as much as it was before. Yes, he wanted to make both Jamal and Leek pay for taking Anika, but some things weren't as worth it as they first seemed.

"They still ghostin'," Marquise informed him. "Jamal's stopped attending his court cases and he's neva out and about anymore. As for Leek, one of the boys spotted him."

"Where?"

"At the burned down warehouse, searchin' through the leftover burnt stuff," Kareem announced.

"Did he see where he went after that?"

"Nah." Kareem shook his head no before adding, "One minute he was there, then the next he was gone."

"They know we lookin' for them," Marquise stated with a frown.

"And they probably lookin' for us too," Blaze responded firmly. "The next time any of our boys spot any one of them on site, tell 'em to shoot them down."

"What?" Kareem queried with confusion. "I thought you wanted to deal with them both."

"I did," Blaze said with a deep sigh, thinking back to Anika's request and his promise. "But I can't."

"But B', they took yo' girl. Surely you must want to deal with them both in the worst possible wa-"

He cut Marq off. "I did Marq, I still do. But I made a promise to Anika not to kill Jamal. She clearly don't want me killin' nobody, so imagine how she'll feel knowin' I killed Leek too. I just gotta learn to let this shit go and move on. I got Anika back, so what's the point?"

"The point is, they plotted against us all and tried to bring our empire down," Kareem snapped, banging his fist on the wooden table in front of him. "Fuck a promise nigga! Those niggas need to pay."

Blaze shot Kareem a rude glare, seeing that he was getting hyped up over the whole situation. He understood his boy's frustrations, but he had to chill.

"Look, I can't break my promise to Anika," Blaze explained. "I'm not like you, 'Reem. I don't keep fuckin' up and makin' my girl pissed."

Kareem kept silent at his harsh words.

"Maybe you ain't even gotta break Nika's promise," Marquise suddenly voiced. "You still got that number for the attorney Jayceon gave you, B'?"

"Yeah, why?"

"I got an idea. I'm not sure if it'll work, but it should," Marquise declared contently. "If I'm right, you won't have to get yo' hands in any blood, Blaze."

"Or Marq and I could just kill both those motherfuckers for ya'," Kareem intervened confidently.

"Nah," Blaze quickly shut him down. "I like Marq's idea better. Tell me more Marq."

Just as Marquise began to explain his sudden theory, one of the Knight Nation boys knocked on the door twice and stepped into the room.

"Yo guys," he greeted them gently.

It was Tyrell, one of the niggas that Blaze had hired a few months back, because he seemed like a hard worker and down for earning some quick cash.

"Sup Ty?" Marq greeted him friendly.

From the blank look now plastered on Tyrell's face, Blaze knew that something was up. He could even feel it as soon as he heard the two knocks on the door.

"Me and a few of the others found somethin' near the back entrance."

"What was it?" Kareem asked.

"I think y'all should come take a look for yo'selves," Tyrell insisted.

So Blaze, Kareem and Marquise got out their seats, made their way out of their main meeting room, and headed to the back entrance of their warehouse.

When they finally arrived, they all noticed the black body bag that had now been unzipped open, allowing the body to be seen.

Blaze instantly caught a glance of the face and he had to do a double take.

"What the fuck?" His question was to no one in particular, so no one answered. Her head had been chopped off from the rest of her body, so in the body bag lay her headless body and her head just lying above. Everyone just looked ahead with shock, at the dead female lying in the body bag.

Masika Brooks.

CHAPTER 13 ~ LOVIN' YOU

"Uh-uh, baby, I don't want yo' ass doin' anythin' right now," Blaze ordered, watching Anika as she lay right next to him. "You stayin' yo' ass in bed."

"But babe, I'm so bored," Anika responded sweetly. "I wanna do something."

"Get some sleep, then me and you can do somethin' to kill our boredom later," he suggested with a smirk.

Finding Masika's body two days ago was definitely a shock, but also an eye opener for Blaze. Leek was no longer the simple minded nigga Blaze made him out to be. He had not only killed his baby mama, but also come on Blaze's turf to drop her body off. The nigga was getting too cocky but Blaze knew that very soon, one way or another, he would be knocked off his high horse.

"Malik, I'm not tired though," she replied, rolling her eyes at him, annoyed at what he was doing. She stared at him only to see his brow raised in the air. "Okay, maybe I am tired… But I had coffee, I'm cool."

She had been up all night, looking for books and tips on something she claimed was for her own personal research. The truth was she didn't want Blaze to know that she had been researching for pregnancy tips, and the different things that could help her have a baby again.

"If you stay in bed, I'll give you a special treat," Malik cajoled, trying to bribe her to stay put. He knew his baby and he knew when she was tired.

"Hmm, and what exactly would that be?" she asked him curiously, with an arched brow.

"Yo' ass stays in bed then you get to find out when you wake up baby."

"Blaze…I really don't want to stay in bed," she concluded simply, before lifting the silk covers off her body. "I'd rather be up doing something… Like being in the kitchen and making us some food maybe."

"Uh-uh." Immediately Blaze was on his feet, running to her bedside. "Baby, just stay in for a bit," he pleaded with her gently before climbing inside the bed next to her. "A nap won't hurt."

"Malik, I do-"

He cut her off, "Shh baby...let's sleep togetha."

"Noooo, I do-"

This time he cut her off with his lips. A quick kiss was all he needed to get her to shut up, then he pulled his lips away from hers. "Sleep for a bit and yo' ass gon' get a big, nice treat."

"I don't want a treat, I wa-...Oh," she quickly realized what he meant by a treat, because Blaze moved one of her free hands underneath the covers to the middle of his sweats, where she was sure she could feel him growing.

"You gon' go to sleep now, so you can get yo' treat when you wake up, right bae?" he questioned her seductively, gently kissing her neck.

"Yes zaddy," she sexily whispered, putting on a seductive accent for him.

Malik wrapped his arms around her and allowed her to place her head on his chest. It took her a few minutes, but she finally drifted off to sleep, leaving him to look down at his pretty woman.

He soon found his eyes shutting and before he knew it, he was sleeping too. He had been pretty tired too, trying to stay awake and watch Anika. She didn't want him staring at her laptop screen, or even knowing what she was researching, but he still wanted to make sure she was straight during the night.

Sleeping was nice. Blaze slept for about an hour and it wasn't until around 1pm when he woke up and noticed Anika had left his arms.

He gently yawned, feeling quite refreshed from the nap that he had just had. Then just as he was about to leave his bed, he turned his head only to see a naked Anika lying close to the edge of the bed. Her back was facing him and her long legs pointed towards him.

"You up daddy?" She turned around momentarily, only to question him and allow him to see a great front view of her body.

"Oh I'm up," he responded cockily. He meant that both in his waking up from his sleep and his dick waking up. Of course he was up. How could he not be?

Within the next couple of seconds, Blaze was completely naked and behind his lady, ready to take things to the next step.

Watching her with her face down and her ass up was a sight that he had definitely missed looking at. Over the past few days, Blaze had been real gentle making love to her, but right now he was willing to change things up a bit, make things more interesting and freaky.

"Malik, I want you… to fuck me with your…big dick, baby," she whispered to him sexily. He couldn't see her facial expressions because her face was down, but he had a feeling that he already knew what look she had in her pretty eyes. The way she spoke made Blaze want to give her exactly what she wanted, with no hesitations. And he planned to do just that.

"Whateva you wan' baby girl," he softly sighed, nudging the soft seal of her pussy before slowly pushing his tip inside of her tight hole. His fingers found their way to hold onto her sides for support, as he pushed his tip further into her pussy. She was so tight for him. Tight, wet, and firm.

"Shit, Malik…" she gently moaned immediately, turning him on even more. He loved the way his government name rolled off her tongue. She was the only person who managed to make him happy when saying that name. He tightened his fingers around her sides, pushing his length between her slick folds, penetrating deeper inside her.

"Fuck," he groaned and rocked his hips into her firm ass, the bed dipping under the shifting weight of their bodies as he thrust his dick inside her soaked pussy to a steady rhythm. The more she moaned, the quicker he filled her up.

Every hard inch of his dick was buried deep between her legs. He spread her legs a little further, allowing her to adjust to his dick filling her fully. She moaned softly when he started rocking back and forth, allowing her to feel each hard ridge and curve of his thickness.

"Blaze… shit, that feels so fucking good," she groaned, tilting her pelvis a little higher so he could push deeper into her pussy.

He dug his fingertips deeper into her sides, forcefully pulling her hips back against his. "Fuck, Nika…baby… This pussy feels so fuckin' good," he groaned. The harder he drove into her, the better it felt. He reached underneath her, wrapping his fingers around her bouncing breasts, leaning into her back more. "Yo' pussy so nice and tight and... Shit," he groaned, squeezing her hard nipples between his fingers.

He started increasing the force and speed in his thrusts, jerking her body harder against his. Her firm ass cheeks collided roughly against his pelvis, creaking the bed springs underneath them. He groaned deep in his throat with each pull of his dick out her pussy.

His lips found their way onto her neck, kissing and sucking at her warm, soft flesh. He loved that he was the only man who was going to be able to make her feel this good, for the rest of her life.

***

Kareem: *"Sadie... Please just talk to me."*

Kareem: *"I just want you to hear a nigga out."*

Kareem: *"U ain't even give a nigga a chance to explain!"*

Kareem: *"I love you."*

Kareem: *"I miss you."*

Kareem: *"Just answer my calls Sadie... Please."*

Kareem: *"I'm sorry."*

Kareem: *"You get the flowers I sent?"*

Kareem: *"I know how much yo' ass loves roses."*

Kareem: *"Baby please, I can't live without you."*

Sadie: *"Die then."*

Sadie knew how petty she was being but truth was, she was too hurt to really speak to Kareem. She wasn't down for hearing his voice or anything, because she knew that hearing him speak would automatically make her want him back. She couldn't lie and say that she didn't miss him. She did. She missed his voice, his face, his touch, his love... Everything.

She still couldn't get over the fact that he had kissed Satin and the way he had been touching her, Sadie couldn't erase the images out of her brain.

She was happy that they were divorced and she had managed to whoop Satin's ass, but she was still pissed. The bitch had touched what no longer belonged to her.

Sadie knew that the more she continued to dwell on the whole situation, the more annoyed she became. There was only one solution to this, and she knew that she needed to do it now sooner than later.

So within the next two hours, she was outside Blaze's golden front door and pressing the bell as rapidly as she could.

She had to get their attention somehow, right? Because for all she knew these love birds could be up to some freaky shit. But right now they had to stop, because Sadie needed her best friend's undivided attention and advice, now more than ever.

When the door swung open, Sadie was greeted to the confused facial expression of her best friend, her sister from another mother, Anika Scott. And the angry facial expression of Blaze standing right behind her.

"Sadie?"

"Hey... Sorry to just pop up like this, but I needed to see you Nika."

"Are you okay?" Anika asked her carefully, seeing the saddened facial expression on her face as Sadie watched Blaze tighten his arms around Anika's waist.

"Yeah I'm... No," she whispered sadly.

Anika broke away from Blaze's arms and stepped closer to Sadie. She already knew what was up. Blaze had told her yesterday. She was just waiting for Sadie to come to her in her own time and talk. She knew she was heartbroken.

"You and 'Reem broke up," Anika commented gently.

Sadie quickly nodded, trying to shake away the tears that were trying to seep through. But it was no use.

"Come to mama, honey," Anika sweetly requested, opening her arms up for Sadie to come into.

Sadie immediately burst into tears and ran into her arms.

"I hate him! I hate him so much!" Sadie sobbed loudly.

"You don't babe, you love him. He fucked up, yes, but you love that nigga," Anika said, stroking her back gently.

"I love him... I love him so much! Why can't I stop loving him, Nika?" Sadie's sobs only continued louder and louder.

She hated feeling this pain.

BAD FOR MY THUG 3: THE FINALE

She hated how much she couldn't stop loving him.

She hated how much she loved Kareem Smith and wanted to spend the rest of her life with that nigga.

CHAPTER 14 ~ DONE DEALS

While Sadie confided in Anika, Blaze decided to give them both some space to talk in private. He understood that Sadie was heartbroken right now and just needed her best friend to give her advice. So he decided to go upstairs into their bedroom, to lay in bed and wait for them to be done.

However, when he made it to the corridor leading to the bedroom, he was instantly diverted by the vibrating phone in his right pocket.

He brought out his iPhone only to see the caller ID as Sergio. He picked up on the second ring.

"Hey jefe," he greeted him warmly. *(Hey boss.)*

"Hola Blaze, ¿cómo estás?" *(Hello Blaze, how are you?)*

"Yo soy un gran jefe. Y tú? *(I'm great boss. And you?)*

"Bien bien. Yo soy un gran resplandor. Y estoy muy bien sabiendo que usted ha llegado a una decisión acerca de mi oferta, sí?" He questioned Blaze curiously. *(Good, good. I'm great Blaze. And I'm great knowing that you've come to a decision about my offer yes?)*

"Tengo jefe," Blaze responded. *(I have boss.)*

"Bien bien. ¿Qué es?" *(Good, good. What is it?)*

"Acepto la oferta. Quiero ser la connexion," Blaze declared. *(I accept the offer. I want to become the connect.)*

"¡Fantástico! Espero verte en Miami de nuevo en un par de semanas que sí?" *(Fantastic! I hope to see you in Miami again in a few weeks yes?)*

"Si jefe," Blaze replied. *(Yes boss.)*

Accepting Sergio's offer wasn't just for himself. Blaze knew that becoming his own connect would not only benefit him, but his wifey too. He had his doubts about the offer before yes, but after some deep thinking Blaze decided that taking this job was for the best. He couldn't pass on this opportunity.

He wasn't sure how Anika would feel about the situation. She had never been aware of the offer because the night that Sergio had brought it up was the same night that she had been taken. So he hadn't actually had a chance to talk to her about it before and he had never brought it up.

She had to be happy, right? Happy knowing that more money was going to be coming into both their lives. She probably wasn't going to be happy about the hours and how much he would be working now all over America, but she would learn to deal with it, right?

Blaze wasn't so sure. He wasn't even sure that he was making the right decision, but whatever is meant to be will be.

Blaze quickly went to his text messages and clicked on the recent group chat message with his boys. Then he messaged them.

Blaze: *"Took the offer from Sergio niggas."*

Kareem: *"Congrats nigga!"*

Marquise: *"Congrats fool!"*

Blaze: *"Thanks y'all. Wish me luck on tellin' Nika though."*

Kareem: *"What, she don't know?"*

Blaze: *"Nah, not yet."*

Marquise: *"Good luck."*

Kareem: *"Gooooood luck."*

Blaze: *"Thanks fools."*

Blaze knew that his boys knew how much work he would have to put into being his own connect. There was no time to be wasted. It was either you get the job done or everyone lost out on profits.

As connect, he would have to be smart and wise. Sergio provided a lot of drugs to a lot of squads moving weight in Atlanta and all over America. A lot of squads that Blaze didn't fuck with and didn't even know of. He would have to be careful in his dealings and not allow his personal feelings of certain niggas to get in the mix.

He had to be a bold, brave and courageous leader. And he certainly couldn't let his brothers or his squad down.

Blaze couldn't help but sigh deeply and begin to contemplate on how he was going to tell Anika about his new job position. Man, he was scared.

The only thing he could think of doing to calm his nerves, was to call his Aunt Ari and to seek some advice from her about the whole situation. So that's exactly what he did.

"Malik, I don't know…. This is a big change from what you usually do."

"But Aunt Ari, it's more money and more opportunity," he announced happily. "I think she'll be okay with it. She'll get used to it eventually."

"You need to take into consideration her feelings too," Ari explained. "How do you think she'll feel knowing you ain't even bother to talk about it with her?"

"She's gotta understand that I'm doin' this for her," Blaze declared. "She can't get mad on a nigga for wantin' to provide for her."

"You're always providing for her, Malik. You've got enough money to feed the whole city of Atlanta. You don't need the money. You good already."

"But I want us to be even better Auntie, I'm only tryin' to do what's best for us and our future."

"And you really believe that workin' more late evenings and being away from Anika more and more, is doing what's best for both of you?" Ari questioned him curiously. "You gotta understand that she will want you to give up this life eventually Malik. You can't be doing it forever. Not now that you got a wife who is going to want to start a big family with you."

"We were on track to startin' our family Aunt… But she lost the baby," he stated sadly.

"What? When was she pregnant?"

"The day she was taken," he slowly began. "She found out that she was pregnant and she lost it while being away."

"Oh my… I'm so sorry, Malik," Ari apologized sympathetically. "I didn't know…"

"I know Aunt, I forgot to tell you. But we've been tryin' for anotha one," Blaze responded. "I want a big family and I know she wan' a big family too. A big family needs to be provided for."

"Okay, you can provide them with money, yes, but you also need to provide them with love and time Malik. If you become connect, how exactly are you gonna have time for your family?"

"I'ma make time…"

"How? You always gon' be workin', where's the time for them?"

"I'on know… But I'ma try my best to always be there for them."

"Always be there for them?" she asked him suspiciously. "Now Blaze, we both know that's not gonna happen very often with you being connect."

When she put it like that, Blaze could see exactly why Anika wouldn't be happy with his new position in the game. And he was only sweating bullets at how he was going to tell her about the whole situation. He didn't want them to end up arguing about it, but he had a feeling that that was exactly what they were going to end up doing.

***

"Blaze, what's up?"

Blaze looked up from his phone and stared into Anika's worried eyes. "Nothin' babe," he lied.

"Are you sure?" she questioned him suspiciously, knowing fully well there was something wrong.

"Actually, there's somethin' I gotta tell you," he stated, shifting closer to her on the loveseat.

"What is it baby?" she asked sweetly, moving one of her hands to stroke his left cheek.

"I recently got a new job offer," he announced with a weak smile.

"Oh okay… Doing what?"

"Well, my connect hit me up, tellin' me 'bout a new spot openin' up… Cause he's retirin'," Blaze said, his weak smile slowly fading at Anika's blank expression.

When she said nothing after his words, he continued to keep speaking. "Well he offered me the spot of becomin' my own connect."

Anika still kept silent.

"So that means more money for me, you and our fa-"

She suddenly cut across him. "Wait, so that means you're taking over his job?"

Blaze reluctantly nodded, seeing her eyes widen with anger.

"Over my dead body you are," she fumed.

"What?" he asked, confused at her words.

"You're not doing it."

"I am, baby, I've already accepted the offe-"

"Without talking to me about it?!" she shouted, getting up from where she sat next to him.

"Baby, I didn't really think you would mind, it's not like we really talk 'bout what I do," he explained.

"You say you want us to get married, but here you are still keepin' secrets away from me, Blaze! What the hell does that tell me about our relationship?"

"Babe," he gently called to her. Seeing her standing up in front of him all fired up, had him suddenly feeling some type of way. A type of way he didn't like. "Just chill, it's not a big deal."

"Not a big deal? Nigga, you're becoming an even bigger drug lord than you are right now," she snapped. "And you tell me that's it's not a big deal? Of course it is! You might not see it as a big deal but I do!"

"You know what I do, Nika," he retorted, getting up from his seat so that he could stand in front of her. "You ain't neva complained 'bout the shit before."

Anika looked up at his towering stance, not intimidated in anyway shape or form. She still planned to hold her ground. "Well I'm complaining now, nigga! If you become connect, you'll never be able to leave the game Malik."

"And why should I? It's what payin' the bills 'round here," he fired back, getting angry at how she was blowing the whole situation out of proportion.

"So you won't ever leave the game for me? You said you would before, Malik!"

"Well a nigga can change his mind, can't he?"

"You know what? Fuck you Malik!"

"Why the hell you hypin' ova some shit that don't need to be hyped ova. Me being connect ain't gon' change shit between us. You actin' as if I'm gon' stop lovin' you or somethin'. I love yo' ass too much to stop fuckin' lovin' you."

"Well if you love me so much…" Her words trailed off, before she added, "You won't take this job Malik."

Malik paused momentarily, staring at her carefully, trying to see if he could find out what was going on with her just by looking into her eyes.

Because she must have been crazy if she thought he wasn't taking this job now.

"I'm takin' it, Anika."

CHAPTER 15 ~ SWEETEST TEMPTATIONS

Anika couldn't believe it.

After all they had been through as a couple, she would think that he would respect her and follow her orders.

But here he stood, telling her that he was taking the job offer and had already accepted it. Anika couldn't stop her shouting now even if she tried. He had her so pissed and hyped up over the whole situation that she didn't even want to hear his voice. All she wanted to hear was her own as she shouted at him and told him how wrong and much of a fool he was for going behind her back and not informing her of the job.

He was moving like a cheater would and Anika didn't like it one bit.

If he claimed that he truly loved her and wanted to spend the rest of his life with her, then why was he keeping secrets from her? She thought they were way past all that and had improved better on their communication, but it seemed like they had not.

She didn't know what to say or do, other than shout at him. And she knew that she wasn't happy with him at all. He had started a fire within her that she now couldn't seem to get out her system.

She knew what being connect would do for Blaze. It might have seemed like a good idea to him, but to her it wasn't. And what pissed her off the most was the fact that he didn't even bother to talk to her about his decision first. He just made it without her, knowing that it wouldn't only affect him. What kind of future husband did that make him?

Blaze decided that the best thing to do, would be to give Anika some space. She was clearly feeling some type of way for no reason at all. And as soon as he confirmed to her that he was taking the job, she lost it.

So Blaze decided to give her space, told her he was going to his club and headed straight there to check on how his business was running. He also decided to text his boys and tell them exactly how shit went down between him and Anika. He already knew they wouldn't find it surprising.

Blaze: *"Told Anika. Went crazy."*

Marquise: *"So I take it she don't want you bein' connect?"*

Blaze: *"Nah."*

Marquise: *"Where you at now?"*

Blaze: *"I had to leave the crib. She was trippin' and I couldn't take it anymore."*

Kareem: *"Where you going?"*

Blaze: *"My club. I'm not tryna hear her shout no more."*

Kareem: *"Man… At least yo' girl still tell you how she feels and shit. Mine won't even talk to me."*

Marquise: *"She gon' come round soon nigga, don't worry."*

Kareem: *"I don't know… I feel like it might be ova between us."*

Blaze: *"It ain't. She was here this afternoon, talkin' to Anika 'bout you."*

Kareem: *"Oh word?"*

Blaze: *"Yeah, she still loves yo' dumb ass."*

Kareem: *"So why won't she talk to me already? Or answer any of my calls."*

Blaze: *"She just needs space."*

Marquise: *"Probably just tryna heal. You know the usual female shit they be doin' all the time. She gon' come round."*

Kareem: *"And if she don't?"*

Marquise: *"Then you gon' have to fight for yo' relationship."*

Blaze: *"Yeah, what he said."*

When entering his strip club, Blaze noticed how packed the club's line was outside and he figured that it was because the best dancer in all of Atlanta was dancing tonight.

He figured right, because when making it to the main show room, he saw her wrapping her long legs around that silver pole and beginning to do all types of freaky shit with it.

Before heading to his office to check the books, he figured a quick watch of Candi dancing couldn't hurt. So he did just that. Besides, he needed to take his mind off the whole situation that had just gone down with Anika.

The more he watched Candi move her half naked body against that silver pole and begin to seduce the crowd with her flexibility, the more enticed and intrigued he found himself becoming. It didn't help that her tits were completely out, and all she wore to cover her body was a black lace thong and on her feet, killer black heels to match.

He hadn't expected to come watch her dance and become so turned on by her. The more he watched her move and perform on stage, the more his bulge began to grow in his pants below.

He knew that the only solution to his current problem was to leave. He couldn't be thinking about fucking a different girl when he had a girl already.

Blaze got up from his seat and headed straight to his office, so that he could focus on checking the club's books.

It was only fifteen minutes after checking the books and being satisfied with the current profits, that a loud knock came from his closed door.

"Come in," he said simply, curious to know who was on the other side.

Unfortunately for him, it was the girl who had managed to make his dick grow within a few seconds of watching her dance on the main stage.

"Hey Blaze," she greeted him happily. "I saw you out there when I was dancin'. I just wanted to come say hello and see if you were good."

"Yeah, I'm good," he lied, before focusing back down on the books laid out in front of him.

"I heard Anika's back now," she announced enthusiastically.

He nodded, avoiding any eye contact with her. Strippers freely walked around topless all the time, but the fact that he was getting turned on by her being topless was a problem.

"You must be so relieved. I know how much she means to yo-"

"Look Candi, what the hell do you wan'? A nigga not really in the mood for all the small talk right now, so cut that shit out. What'chu want?" he questioned her, not in the mood for talking about Anika right now.

BAD FOR MY THUG 3: THE FINALE

"Well, what I really want..." she said, now sauntering closer to his desk. When she made it round to him, she sat on the edge of his desk and lifted his chin up so he was forced to stare into her eyes. And everything else below her eyes. "...Is you, Blaze."

"You know I'm taken, Candi," he reminded her. "What makes you think I want you?"

"Because I've seen the way you look at me, Blaze," she commented with a sexy smirk. "I know how much I turn you on."

"And what makes you think that ma'?"

"Cause I know how hard my dancin' got your dick," she announced, lifting her hand to the middle of his pants. Blaze looked down curiously at the way she was now stroking his big bulge through his pants.

He couldn't lie and say the shit didn't feel good, because it sure did. The more she stroked, the harder he became and he couldn't help but quietly groan at how good it felt. Every stroke was only melting the stress and frustration that he had been feeling before. Man... Every stroke only enticed and seduced him more.

"You want me Blaze and I'ma show you how much you want me."

Within the next five minutes, Blaze's pants and boxers had been pulled to the ground, and before he could try to stop her, she was already wrapping her smooth lips around his thick head.

"Candi... Shit, stop..." He attempted to tell her to stop.

But it was no use. Her tongue was on him, and she had officially found out his weakness.

Bomb ass head.

She smiled to herself before peeking her tongue through her lips, dragging the tip of her tongue up along his hard shaft.

"Mmmm," she purred, licking her lips. She dropped her tongue back to the base of his tool and flattened her entire tongue against his length, slowly dragging her tongue back up his thickness.

"You don't want me too, though," she declared, holding his tense gaze. She repeated the same slow lick, then, quickly further parting her lips, she pulled his shaft deeper into her mouth, not wasting anytime to suck him.

"Shit... Oh God," Blaze groaned, feeling Candi work her magic on his dick and watching her intense gaze. "Fuck..." He reached down to slip his fingers through her long, straight blonde hair. He couldn't help it. It was a habit of his that he had yet to overcome.

Her lips sealed tighter around him, pressing her tongue back underneath his length, Candi pulled back, sucking hard, until her lips reached the smooth head of his dick. She swirled her tongue around the tip of his length before pushing her head back down on his dick.

Keeping a firm grasp at the hard base of his dick, Candi started stroking him while bobbing her head up and down, using her lips to pull hard up and down, on his dick. Her free hand dug into his thigh, pulling his dick deeper into her mouth.

"Fuuck," he murmured, impressed by Candi's skills to make him feel so good, so effortlessly. She was driving him crazy and he knew that there was no way he could get her to not finish what she had started.

She rapidly flicked her tongue against the sensitive underside of his dick, then swirled her tongue around it.

"Goddamn..."

Then, her lips suddenly popped off and she pushed her chest forward, clinging onto her big tits as she instantly began using them both to rub against his dick.

It was as if she had taken a class on all his weaknesses when it came to the bedroom, because she knew all the right things to do. But watching the way she was so bent on pleasuring him, made him suddenly realize that this wasn't the chick he wanted on her knees for him. This wasn't the chick that he wanted to spend the rest of his life with.

"Candi," he firmly called out to her, grabbing hold of her right shoulder and alerting her to stop massaging her breasts over his dick. "I don't wan' this, you need to stop now."

"What, why?"

"This shit was a mistake, you not the girl I wan' to spend the rest of my life with."

"Stop playin' Blaze, you was lovin' me suckin' on your dick just now," she commented confidently. "You want this." And she tried to continue pleasuring him again, but Blaze was certain on his decision as he held her back.

"Chill Candi, I'on want you. This was a big mis-"

And that's when the office door suddenly flung open.

A loud gasp came from the door. Malik looked straight ahead only to be completely shocked and feeling like he suddenly wanted to cry.

Standing in the doorway was Anika. Her mouth open and her eyes observing the scene that lay ahead.

A topless Candi on her knees in between Blaze's legs.

A guilty Blaze, with his dick out and all eyes on Anika.

Anika didn't bother staying for the details any longer. She decided to leave the cheater and his new sweetest temptation. It was obvious that instead of fixing things between them, Blaze would rather start fucking around with his stripper. And that was absolutely fine with Anika. She was done.

"Baby, I swear this shit ain't my fault!"

Anika quickly walked away.

CHAPTER 16 ~ HEARTS BROKEN

Each tear that continued to fall down her cheeks was quickly pushed away by her shaky hands. She was trying so hard to fight back the tears, while she quickly drove back to Blaze's mansion to get her things.

Now as she packed her things into each of her designer suitcases, the tears wouldn't stop falling. Why wouldn't they stop falling? She was tired of this everlasting pain that wouldn't stop hurting her. Why couldn't it just all stop? She didn't want to feel like this.

How could he do this to her? How could he run away from their relationship only to head straight to the next bitch's arms, in this case, mouth? How could he fuck up what they had built so well together?

Anika didn't want to think about anything to do with him anymore. All she knew was that she was done with this relationship. She wasn't about to let herself go through the humiliation again of Blaze's infidelity. If he wanted to be with someone else, then that was cool. He could go do that and leave her the hell alone.

The sudden slam of the entrance door downstairs immediately caught Anika by surprise. She was hoping that she would have packed quick enough to not have him meet her here, but hearing his fast, loud footsteps running up his stairs, told her that she was still going to have to leave regardless of him being here.

"Anika!" Blaze frantically called out to her, expecting to hear some sort of reply but he realized how bad he had fucked up before, and she was definitely not going to talk to him.

But what he didn't expect was to see her packing her things once he entered their bedroom.

"Baby, what... what'chu doin'?" he questioned her, slowly stepping deeper into the room. He hoped she wasn't thinking of doing what it looked like she was doing, because he wasn't letting her out their bedroom door. Not until they talked about things.

Not once did she look up at him, she only continued to quickly pack her clothes. She didn't even acknowledge his presence. Blaze noticed the tears falling down her cheeks and he was fast on his heels, moving closer to her.

He reached out his hands to hold her before saying, "Anika, bae, I'm so-"

"Don't fucking touch me," she spat, pushing him away from her. "You stupid, lying cheater!"

"Look, I know I made a mistake Nika, but I swear I didn't even want her. She knew I was down and used that shit to her advantage! She seduced me and I admit I almost fell for it, baby... But not completely."

Anika kept silent as she zipped her suitcase. What was the point of listening to his side of things when she knew she was leaving him still? It didn't matter what he said to try and fix things. Shit was unfixable because she was done with him.

"Nika, I swear I don't feel anythin' for her! She's a fuckin' stripper, why the hell would I fee-"

"She's a stripper at your club because you hired her, nigga! You've probably been attracted to her for years," she snapped. "You've probably fucked her before."

"We neva fucked. I swear!" he shouted back. "I'm not even attracted to her the way I'm attracted to you Anika!"

"Well, you must be pretty fuckin' attracted to her to let her bring out your dick and start sucking it!" she fumed, pointing at him angrily.

"I stopped her though, Anika," he stated tensely. "I knew that the shit was wrong because I didn't want to step out on you, I love you."

"Well con-fucking-gratulations, nigga," Anika sang in a happy tone, lifting the handle of one of her cases. "You've done just that and I'm leaving your dumb ass!"

"No you ain't," he retorted, grabbing onto her handle to try to stop her from leaving. "I'm not lettin' you go."

"Says the one who left and let another bitch touch what is supposed to only belong to me!"

"I'm sorry Anika, fuck! How many times do I have to fuckin' apologize?"

"You apologizing won't change shit," she declared. "It's over between us. I'm not doing this anymore."

"You not doin' what anymore?" he asked her curiously. "You not doin' the fact that you love me and you want to spend the rest of yo' life with me? You not doin' the fact that regardless of this shit goin' on now, we are meant to be together?"

"No," she said rudely. "I'm not doin' the lies and the secrets anymore, Malik!"

"What lies?"

"You lying and keeping secrets away from me. You couldn't tell me about the job offer from Sergio and you didn't even discuss it with me, your ex-future wife, before taking it. I'm tired of being played."

"I neva played you, Nika," he responded. "I did nothin' but love and look after you. That's all I've ever done since we been together. Tried my hardest to look after and protect you."

"Well clearly you didn't look after me or protect me well enough, because who was the one that got kidnapped? Remember that."

"Of course I remember that shit, Anika! Who do you think was lookin' for you twenty-four fuckin' seven and cryin' every single day, knowin' that I didn't have a single fuckin' clue where you were!"

"None of this shit would have happened in the first damn place, if you weren't a fuckin' drug lord!" she shouted furiously.

"So this is all my fault now?" he queried with a frown.

"Yes!" she exclaimed. "This is all your fault!"

"But it ain't my fault when I'm buyin' yo' ass all the shit you want, all the designer shit you love, makin' you happy, dickin' you down. It ain't my fault then, is it?"

"It's all your fault, Malik," she pushed. "Because you're too addicted and obsessed with this game. You won't ever leave it, even if I tried to force you to."

"Me bein' in the game is what pays the bills around here, Anika," he snapped. "Me being in the game is what makes yo' ass fuckin' happy daily. Where do you think the money to fund yo' luxuries come from?"

"You won't ever le-"

He cut her off. "You knew what I did from the start of this fuckin' relationship. And you were cool with it too! Yo' ass neva once complained. Now you talkin' about when a nigga gon' leave the game, but you neva say this shit when I'm fuckin' you! Or when I'm buyin' you all the shit you want, when I'm makin' you happy! Now you wan' have an attitude after all the shit I've done for yo' ass. All the time I've sacrificed for you! I've done so much for you, because I love you! I've been in love with you since the second I laid eyes on you. Fuck all those other bitches, I'm yours, Nika! Only thing that ever mattered to me was you and my niggas!"

"You loved me, but you cheated on me with Desiree," Anika said, reminding him of the past. "You say fuck all these bitches but you stay fucking them."

"Why you bringin' up old shit?" he rudely queried. "Shit that don't fuckin' matter anymore. I'm with you, ain't I?"

"You may be with me, but deep down you always been a cheater at heart, Malik! Admit it!"

"I ain't neva been a cheater at heart," he explained. "It's not my fault chicks always want me. That's just the way shit's always been. I can't do nothin' to stop that. But I can do somethin' to make sure that I'm loyal to the woman I love. And that's you, Anika!"

"Well, clearly you ain't been loyal enough," she said. "If you were loyal, I wouldn't have caught you with your dick out with the stripper that works at your club, on her knees for you! If you were loyal, you wouldn't have taken the job offer without hearing my opinion of things."

"So I ain't loyal, yet I'm the one that looked for you and brought you home."

"You were supposed to do that!" she loudly shouted. "I was taken and it was your obligation to bring me back home."

"I could have left you though, I could have forgotten all 'bout you and just decided to go with some next chick," he retorted. "I could have let the temptations of yo' ass bein' away from me, get to me."

"So why didn't you then?"

"Because I love you, Anika!" he yelled. "Are you not fuckin' listenin' to anythin' a nigga is sayin' to you right now?"

"I am listening, but all I keep hearin' is shit that don't matter anymore. Because it doesn't change what's happened. And it won't fix the shit between us now."

"Why can't it change shit between us, Anika? You just so fuckin' stubborn that you can't see that we can fix things and we can move forward from all this."

"Nothing would have to be fixed in the first place if you weren't so obsessed and addicted with shit that doesn't matter anymore. You've got almost all the money in the world, why the hell do you need even more?"

"You keep complain' about shit that doesn't have anythin' to do with our relationship. You thinkin' of leavin' me right now, is what the problem is now. You complain, but you won't complain about stayin' and trying to work things out. Complainin' 'bout me being obsessed with the game, won't change shit Anika! Bein' in the game is my job, it's what I do and you just gon have to accept it."

She kept silent for a few seconds before concluding, "Well, since I'm complaining so much now, then you should just let me go. Stop controlling me all the time. Let me leave and you can continue to do whatever the fuck you want to do."

Blaze knew that going back and forth with her wasn't getting them anywhere. She was so hell bent on leaving and no matter what he said to try and change her mind, she wasn't going to budge.

So he let her go.

Seeing her walk out the door, suitcases in both hands, had him feeling like his heart was being snapped into little, tiny pieces. He didn't want her to leave him. She wasn't ever supposed to leave him. But here they were.

After hearing the front door downstairs slam close, Malik's tears slowly started to leave his eyes.

How was he supposed to live without her?

***

"Why have we waited so long, Jamal? We should have murked all those niggas by now," Leek commented, watching as Jamal poured himself a shot of whiskey.

"You know why we waited," Jamal responded calmly. "Give them a little power and confidence and it'll have them going crazy. And then we-"

"Then we strike," Leek interrupted him, finishing off his words for him. "I know, I know but when do we strike? I'm tired of those niggas thinkin' they winnin'."

"We strike very soon," Jamal replied. "We all know there's a war coming. And they probably think they gon' be ready, but they won't be. Don't worry, we got this."

"What about Anika? You still want her?"

Jamal contemplated to himself for a while before speaking, "Never really did. But once I realized that she was Blaze's, I just knew that takin' her would be a good advantage. That was until he managed to take her back."

"Yeah, I know… All because of fuckin' Masika."

"You've handled that right?"

"Yeah," Leek stated confidently. "She's definitely been handled alright."

"Good, good. Now we focus on making sure those niggas get handled. It's time to end this shit once and for all."

"Yep," Leek agreed. "Once and for all."

***

Anika quickly ran up the steps leading to Sadie's apartment. She had left her cases in the trunk of her car, because she wasn't in the mood to be carrying her things up right now. They only reminded her of why she had left in the first place and who she had left.

Once making it to the front of her door, Anika gently knocked twice.

"Nika?"

The door swung open and Anika was greeted by the curious eyes of her best friend.

"I left Blaze," she announced before suddenly bursting into tears.

"Aww honey," Sadie cooed to her sweetly before pulling her into her warm embrace. "Come to mama."

CHAPTER 17 ~ TROUBLE IN PARADISE

"You go first…"

"Okay, well, you know how I found him, kissing up on her and the bitch dressed in nothing but lingerie," Sadie began. "We haven't talked for a few weeks now. He kept on texting me and calling me, but I just kept on ignoring him."

"Do you think you're going to get back with him?" Anika queried curiously.

"Umm… I don't know," Sadie admitted. "I won't lie, I miss him and I love him. I honestly can't see myself being with anyone else but him right now."

"So why won't you get back with him?"

"I don't want to be the one to get us back together," Sadie responded. "I know it makes me seem petty, but that's just the way I feel. And I'm still not really in the best of mood to talk to him, so really and truly I'm not sure how it's all going to go. The whole situation with Satin just took me completely off guard. But enough about me, you've still yet to tell me about why you left Blaze."

Anika took a deep breath before explaining the whole situation to Sadie. From finding out about his job offer from Sergio, the first argument, Blaze leaving to give her some space, her wanting to sort things out with him, finding him with Candi, heading home to pack and the final confrontation between them.

"Wait, Candi? Stripper Candi?"

Anika nodded sadly.

"That bitch was probably after him the whole time," Sadie stated with a frown. "I'm not justifying what he did, but it does sound like she seduced him."

"I know, Sadie, but he still should have stopped her from the second she started. He shouldn't have let it get to the point of her being able to pull down his pants and bring his shit out," Anika explained. "Seduced by her or not, he's still in the wrong. And we've been through this shit before. You remember Desiree?"

"Oh yeah, I remember her," Sadie responded.

"That whole situation took me a few weeks to recover from, you remember how upset I was."

"And stubborn, too. Yeah, I remember."

"Stubborn?" Anika queried with an arched brow.

"Yes stubborn, Nika," Sadie pushed. "You know how stubborn you are. I know you can't help it sometimes, but that's just the way you've always been."

"But sometimes even being stubborn doesn't work. He's fucked up our relationship again," Anika commented.

"But don't forget the fact that he loves you Anika. He loves you more than anything in the world," Sadie reminded her gently. "He would do anything for you."

"No he wouldn't," Anika said. "He won't leave the game for me."

"Maybe if you asked him to leave in a different way, then he would. And you need to remember that he's been in the game almost all his life. It's all he really knows. It's his way of earning money and I think now that he has you, he's probably thinking that he needs to work ten times harder to make sure you're always good. That's how much he cares about you, Nika."

"But he doesn't need to work ten times harder," Anika stated. "He's good, I'm good – we're good. I'd rather he not take the offer and focus on working on us."

"Then you need to communicate that to him, honey," Sadie advised.

"I know... But I'd rather just have some space away from him though," Anika voiced. "I need time to think and decide if being with him is really the right thing to do."

"And how is it not? You love him, he loves you. You guys just need to communicate and I'm sure you'll be fine. But hey, I guess you do need space away from him... I mean, space away from 'Reem has really allowed me to think about what's best for me."

"And have you decided what's best for you yet?"

"Well... Yes and no," Sadie said quietly. "I'll see how things go."

"You know, for someone who gives really good advice, you should really take your own."

Sadie chuckled lightly. "I know, I know... But sometimes feelings get in the way of all that."

Anika smiled at her best friend, thankful that she had her in her life. If she didn't have Sadie, who else would give her such great advice? And who would be willing to let her crash at their house for as long as she needed?

"So, what are we gonna do now?" Anika curiously asked.

"Get some food and alcohol while we watch a movie?"

"Sounds like a great plan," Anika said with excitement.

***

Marquise placed the bottle of whiskey in the center of the wooden table where the boys all sat around, and placed the three glasses in front of everyone.

Blaze was the first one to grab the bottle and pour himself a large amount that reached the tip of his glass. Then he lifted the glass to his lips and swung it all down in one whole chug.

"Damn nigga," Kareem called out to him. "Slow down, we just got here."

"He needs it," Marquise stated simply. "We all do with the shit we been going through."

"All 'cause of these females... Man, I'm sick of feelin' like this," Kareem explained. "Sadie still hasn't come round despite all the space I've given her, and I just don't know what the fuck to do anymore."

"How long has it been since y'all last spoke?" Blaze queried suddenly.

"More than two weeks," Kareem stated sadly. "She won't answer a nigga's calls or reply to my texts. She only replied once when I told her that I can't live wit'out her."

"What she say?" Marquise queried.

"She said 'Die then'."

"Damn that's cold," Marquise exclaimed with a scoff.

"Ice cold," Blaze mumbled as he reached for the whiskey bottle again.

"I've given her all the space she wants and she still don't wan' a nigga? We can't keep doin' this shit. We either togetha or we not."

"You love her, right?" Marquise asked.

Kareem quickly nodded.

"Then just give her some more space. She's probably missin' yo' ass and she gon' come 'round soon. Don't worry, just leave her alone for some more," Marquise advised simply.

"I hope you right nigga, I'm tired of waitin'. I wan' her back already, I miss her."

"What happened wit' you and Anika, B'?"

Blaze looked up at Marquise's curious hazel eyes, only to sigh deeply at the thought of explaining the shit that went down with him and Anika. Thinking about it all the time only made him depressed.

"We had an argument about the job offer from the connect," he began with a frown. "I decided to give her space, so I left to go to my club. Candi came to see me and before a nigga knew it, she was on her knees suckin' me off and titty fuckin' me."

"What?!" Marquise immediately burst into laughter.

"What's funny, fool?" Blaze wasn't liking the way he was suddenly laughing at him. What the hell was funny?

"It's the way yo' ass said titty..." His words trailed off as he burst into laughter again.

"That's not even the best part," Blaze snapped tensely. "Anika came in once I had managed to stop her. Then she was rushin' back home and packin' her shit up."

"Did you not try and stop her?" Kareem asked.

"Of course, I tried to stop her, but we ended up arguin' even more and she just pissed me off completely. We weren't gettin' anywhere so I let her go, and we ain't talked since."

"Damn... That's cold," Marquise commented.

"Ice cold," Kareem said. "So what'chu finna do now?"

"Just givin' her ass some space."

"And if she doesn't come 'round?" Kareem curiously queried.

"She gon' come 'round," Blaze responded. "She know we supposed to be togetha. She know how much I love her and she know how much she loves me. I'ma just give her some space and hope for the best.

There ain't no point in me forcin' her to come back, she gotta do that shit on her own."

"Yeah, I guess you right nigga," Kareem agreed.

"Compared to all y'all niggas, my problem seems like shit."

"What, you and Naomi, right?" Blaze asked.

"Yeah, yeah... She found out that her best friend and her husband were fuckin' 'round behind her back. So she been stayin' 'round mine, but she's always fuckin' cryin' and I just don't know what the hell to do."

"It's probably a huge shock to her now, knowin' that they were sneakin' 'round her back. That's probably why she keeps cryin'," Kareem suggested.

"She found them fuckin'," Marquise revealed.

"Woah... what?" Blaze couldn't believe it.

"On their shared bed," Marquise continued. "They got kids together, but they went to summer camp for two weeks, and Naomi decided to spend the two weeks with me. When she came to see me, I told her I was taking her away for a few days. So she decided that she didn't have the right clothes and shit. I took her to her crib the next day, waited for her to get her shit and she came out in tears. Her best friend had followed her out, tryin' to explain shit, and her husband came out too."

"And what did you do?" Kareem questioned him suspiciously.

"Wait, huh? How you know I did somethin'?"

"We know you did somethin'. Ain't no way you just stayed in that fuckin' car and watched," Blaze announced. "What yo' ass do?"

"Of course I did somethin'!" Marquise exclaimed with a grin. "How could I not? She been tryin' to come to a decision about who she was goin' to choose and I just knew it was gon' be me. So I got out the car, opened the door for her and when that nigga saw me, he started askin' the dumbest questions and tellin' her to get out the car. Then he called her a whore. I lost it after that."

"You fucked him up?"

"Yup," Marquise stated happily. "You know how I get down, B'. I don't like niggas disrespectin' what belongs to me. So I had to teach his ass a lesson. End of story. But only for a bit though, Naomi stopped me."

"Awww man," Kareem groaned. "Why didn't you call us up? That would have been fun to watch."

"Fun?" Blaze's brow rose up with surprise. "Now you know damn well we would have got involved, 'Reem."

"Hmm... Yeah, probably."

"But yeah, she's left him now and now she's wit' me," Marquise declared.

"Are you happy?" Kareem questioned his boy curiously.

"Kinda... I'll be happy when she finally divorces his ass though."

"Well at least you got somethin' good goin' on compared to 'Reem and I," Blaze said. "We just gotta pray that things get better in our relationships."

"And they will niggas, don't worry 'bout it. Just give them the space, they love you both, they'll come running," Marquise advised before deciding to switch the subject. "What we need to be worryin' 'bout is Leek and Jamal."

"They still hidin'," Kareem stated. "They gon' come out soon though. They can't be hidin' foreva."

"I already told y'all niggas 'bout my promise to Nika, right?"

Both Kareem and Marquise nodded.

"Yeah, we remember it B', don't you worry. Besides, with the attorney helpin' us, I'on think we'll need to even kill Jamal," Marquise explained.

"And our real main focus is just endin' all this bullshit once and for all. No more of these fools comin' for us, we ain't got the time for it anymore," Kareem added.

"Exactly," Blaze agreed. "It's time for us to just focus on the future. If Anika wants me to leave the game soon, then I gotta be ready to leave. I can't be beefin' with niggas that aren't doin' anythin' but causin' problems. We get rid of them and then we good."

"And if Sadie wants me to do the same, I gotta be ready too."

"Same with Naomi... If our ladies wan' us to go, we gotta leave knowin' the nation is left in good hands."

They all nodded in agreement before lifting their glasses up in the air, toasting to the Knight Nation and the future with their baes.

All Blaze wanted was his baby back. There was no better time than when he was with her. He couldn't control the temptations when he wasn't with her before, but he knew that he could now. Fuck all those bitches, he was hers. He wasn't going to fuck shit up between them ever again. She wanted to be done with him, but he was sure that her heart wouldn't let her leave him.

She wanted him and he wanted her.

CHAPTER 18 ~ STRIKE THREE

"Estoy declinar la oferta de jefe," Blaze informed Sergio contently. *(I'm declining the offer boss.)*

"¿Qué, qué hijo?" *(What, why son?)*

"Tengo demasiado en juego en este momento para estar lidiando con ser uno de los mayores conecta en toda América," Blaze responded simply. *(I got too much at stake right now to be dealing with being one of the biggest connects in the whole of America.)*

"¿Es tu mujer?" *(Is it your woman?)*

"Sí ... Pero también sé que el ser de conexión no es la opción correcta para mí ahora. Estoy tratando de dejar el juego pronto, no ser atrapado en ella el jefe más profundo. *(Yes... But I also know that bein' connect isn't the right choice for me now. I'm tryin' to leave the game soon, not be stuck into it deeper boss.)*

"Te escucho hijo. Es debido a mi mujer también que me estoy retirando. Ella no me quiere en este negocio más," Sergio explained. *(I hear you son. It's because of my woman too that I'm retiring. She don't want me in this business anymore.)*

"Sí ... Y nos encanta a los dos tanto que estamos dispuestos a hacer cualquier cosa para que sean felices." *(Yeah... And we love them both so much that we're willin' to do anythin' to make them happy.)*

"Exactamente," Sergio said in agreement. *(Exactly.)*

After making Sergio aware of his decision, Blaze decided to let his boys know what he had done too.

Blaze: *"Spoke to Sergio."*

Kareem: *"So he know 'bout you not takin' the offer now?"*

Blaze: *"Yeah, he does."*

Marquise: *"A'ight."*

Marquise: *"It's for the best though. Anika don't want you doin' that and you gotta respect her wishes."*

Blaze: *"Yup."*

Kareem: *"You heard from her yet?"*

Blaze: *"Nah."*

Blaze: *"You heard from Sadie?"*

Kareem: *"Nah."*

Blaze: *"You know they togetha right?"*

Kareem: *"How you know?"*

Blaze: *"Anika ain't got no family but her. They definitely togetha."*

Kareem: *"Guess we just gotta keep givin' them space."*

Blaze: *"Yeah... Space."*

Blaze was fine with giving Anika space right now. He knew she was missing him, just as much as he missed her. He couldn't stop thinking about her, and how sorry he was for hurting her. All he ever wanted to do was make her happy.

"You like it baby?" he asked with an arched brow, already knowing her answer.

Anika kept silent. Instead she slowly walked up to him and once standing in front of him, she looked up and branded her soft lips to his.

The kiss was heaven on earth for Blaze. One thing he loved doing, was kissing his lady, Anika Scott. Not only was she a great kisser, she knew how to enchant him from the very first swirl of her tongue against his. He loved the way she kissed, tasted and danced their mouths together.

Both her arms went around his neck and his arms went around her slim, curvy waist, pulling her closer to him. His hands found their way to her ass cheeks and firmly began to squeeze, while moving her away from her new closet and back towards his bed.

Their lips momentarily pulled off each other's, so Blaze could talk to her.

"You like it?"

"I love it Malik, thank you so much," she sweetly thanked him.

"You gon' show me how much you love it?"

Anika nodded sexily, before moving from in front of Blaze to behind him. She roughly pushed him, making him fall back onto his red, king-sized bed, causing it to gently bounce.

He looked up at her, with a wild look of excitement now in his grey eyes. He could tell she was about to dominate him, bringing out the freaky side of hers that he had grown to love so much. His freaky Anika.

"Take your boxers off," she ordered firmly. "Now."

And he couldn't forget about how happy and good they were when they worked on their communication together.

"I gotta go," he whispered as he gently pecked her lips. "I ain't wan' yo' ass to get angry when you woke and saw that I ain't here."

"Why you gotta go so soon Malik?" she asked sadly, only making Blaze smile happily at the fact that she didn't want him going anywhere. Even though they had spent the last four days together, she still didn't want him to leave.

"Girl, I gotta go," he explained. "I wish I could stay but I got business to take care of."

She sighed softly but still kept a saddened facial expression.

"I'll be back before you know it beautiful," he promised lovingly. "A'ight?"

"Okay," she mumbled, still eyeing him sadly.

"Hey, don't give me that look bae," he whispered. "I'll be back before you know it and spend the rest of my time with yo' pretty ass and no one else."

She nodded stiffly, watching as he lifted her hand to his lips so he could softly kiss it. She smiled at the romantic gesture, but Blaze knew his baby all too well to know that she still wasn't happy.

So he laid back down on her bed, fully clothed, and made her sit on his torso so that he could stare directly into her pretty eyes when he questioned her. This was something new that he was going to do with her all the time from now on. It would be their intimate confession time and a way for them to truthfully tell each other how they were feeling. Also, by looking into each other's eyes, Blaze knew that it would be hard for him to lie and her to lie, because the other person would easily know.

"So talk to me," he requested. "Tell me what's up wit'chu."

"Nothing Malik," she stated quietly, watching as his brow arched up in the air, clearly not believing her.

He slowly began stroking the side of her warm thigh as he spoke. "I know somethin' botherin' you beautiful. I'm yo' man, you can talk to me, 'bout anythin'. I'm listenin', I promise I won't get mad at whatever it is. I'm listenin'."

"Okay. Well..."

Honesty was key in a relationship and in order for their relationship to last forever, Blaze was about that honesty. So listening to her be honest about her fears of him leaving her and cheating on her again, and her silly insecurities of not being good enough for him, meant that Blaze couldn't get mad.

Even though he was mad that she was worrying about bullshit, he still remained cool. All he could do was be a good listener and be the best man possible, by trying to assure her of his love and loyalty to her.

Now all he wanted was her to back by his side, so they could work on their relationship and so he could ensure her that he wasn't going to fuck up again.

He had fired Candi. He didn't care that she was one of the best strippers in the whole of Atlanta. He didn't care about how much revenue she brought into the club. She wasn't important. What was important was Anika. And he didn't want any more temptations from Candi.

While reminiscing on Anika, Blaze's smartphone began to vibrate in his back pocket and he pulled it out, hoping to see the caller ID display her name, but instead it was Auntie Ari's.

He was slightly disappointed but quickly got over it when he realized that he hadn't spoken to her in quite some time.

"Aunt?"

"Malik," she greeted him warmly. "How you been?"

"I've had better days," he admitted.

"Why, what's going on? What've you done to Nika this time?"

"Huh, why you think I done some shit?" he asked curiously.

"Because you my nephew and I know you," she explained with a light chuckle. "What've you done?"

"She caught me with Candi, but I swear it wasn't on purpose. I was seduced," Blaze revealed.

"Candi, the stripper?"

"Yeah, she started sucking my d-"

BAD FOR MY THUG 3: THE FINALE

"Umm, ewe. Spare me the details, Malik," Ari cut across him with disgust. "Is that the only reason why she left you?"

"How you know she left me Auntie?" Blaze was confused as to how Auntie Ari knew everything that was going on between him and Anika without him telling her the story. She had to be psychic or something.

"The minute you picked up the phone and I heard your voice boy, I knew some shit had gone down. Now that you tellin' me she caught your dumb ass with a stripper, I know she must have left you," Ari announced.

"Yeah, you right," Blaze said sadly. "She left me. She found out about the job offer I got from Sergio to be connect, I took it wit'out speakin' to her first 'cause I figured she'll be okay with it. But apparently she wasn't... And I know you warned me about her not being happy 'bout it before, but I thought you would be wrong and she'd be okay wit' it all."

"Why'd you figure she'd be okay with it in the first place Malik?"

"She knew what I did the minute we started fuckin' 'round with each other. She know that me doin' this is my way of bein' able to provide her with all the shit she wants and more. So I thought she wouldn't care about me being connect and she would just see it as more income for the both of us."

"And now you see that she loves you for you and not for your money, or what you can do for her," Ari gently voiced. "You were so used to being with Masika and always giving her money and materialistic things because that's what she wanted from you. She was in love with all the wealth and success you brought into her life. But now you got a girl who doesn't care about all that, Malik. She cares about you as a person and loves you. All that other stuff is just a bonus for her, but it ain't important."

"I hear you Aunt, and I get all that now. But she's not talkin' to me right now so I'ma just give her all the space she wants."

"I guess that's for the best right now. She needs it and I think you do too. You've been so invested into finding her and now that you've found her, I think you need that break and a chance to see that she's gonna be okay without you."

"I hear ya' Aunt," he responded. "How you been though? How's the fam?"

MISS JENESEQUA

"I'm good, everyone's good. I'm thinkin' 'bout having the barbeque in two weeks, think you'll be down to come with Anika?"

"Yeah, I'on see why not," he replied.

"Bring Marq and 'Reem too. Y'all should all come with your girls."

"Sounds like a plan," he said with a soft sigh.

"Guess I'll see you soon Malik," Ari concluded.

"Yeah, see ya' soon Aunt, thanks for callin'."

Five minutes after ending the phone call with his Aunt, Blaze was feeling sleepy and figured a nice nap would be cool right now. However, within a few seconds of him walking towards his bedroom, his phone began to vibrate in his hand.

He lifted his phone only to see Kareem calling him. He reluctantly picked up on the third ring.

"Yo?"

"Blaze! Yo, you need to get down to the main warehouse right now," Kareem revealed, sounding fearful and upset.

"Why, what's u-"

"Leek. Jamal," Kareem stated in a frustrated tone.

"What about them?" he queried, getting worried at the way Kareem sounded.

"They set the warehouse on fire."

Blaze immediately ended the call and was fast on his feet into his bedroom to get dressed to leave.

The main warehouse was where most of the Knight Nation's ammo and drugs were. If it had been set on fire that meant all their weapons and 70% of their supply was going to be gone. The idea of it had Blaze burning up with anger, as he began to place his feet into Timberland boots.

He just hoped that the warehouse wasn't completely damaged and some of the boys were able to save the building.

However, once making it to the warehouse, Blaze was astonished.

"They tried to save it," Kareem revealed. "But then it just went up in flames. Had to have a bomb up in there or somethin'."

BAD FOR MY THUG 3: THE FINALE

The whole entire building was blown to the ground. All that was left was rubble and the remains of the building. All their ammo, drugs... *Gone.*

Blaze had been angry many times in his life, but this event right here blew everything out the water. Of course the Knight Nation had other warehouses around Atlanta, but there was a reason for having a main warehouse. This was the first warehouse that had ever been set up. Blaze, Kareem and Marquise had worked so hard over the years to make things good and solid at this warehouse, so to see it burnt down to the ground right now was extremely painful for them all.

This shit had to end once and for all. The first strike had been the attacks on the Knight Nation, the second strike had been taking Anika, and the third strike had been destroying their main warehouse.

Three strikes and they were now out.

CHAPTER 19 ~ NEW WAR

Blaze couldn't speak. No words would dare leave his lips. He knew that if he spoke, no nice words would be coming out. So he decided to keep still and silent as he listened to Marquise and Kareem talk through the plan.

"Yeah, so the attorney has the documents…"

How could Leek and Jamal do this shit? All the hard work that had been put into the warehouse was now completely down the drain. And it angered him so much, but he knew he had to remain calm and stick to the plan.

"Blaze, you good nigga?"

Blaze looked up at 'Reem only to nod. "Yeah, I'm good."

"I know how much the warehouse meant to you," Marquise said. "How much it meant to us all. Especially because of how hard we worked on making it solid and filled with all the stock that helped us become better ova the years."

"Yeah, and we definitely had a lot of good memories ova there," Kareem stated coolly. "I'ma miss it."

"We got the others though," Marquise reminded the boys. "They not as big, but we could get some renovations done or some shit."

Blaze simply nodded at his boys, agreeing with all they had said. He knew he would soon get over the whole situation with the main warehouse and he would be able to focus on the plan of taking Jamal and Leek down.

"Jamal's the brains behind The Lyons' whole operation," Marquise explained. "Without him, they just regular ass niggas, with no proper expertise on the streets and what to do against us. Notice how mediocre those niggas were when Jamal wasn't 'round?"

"Oh yeah, I remember. They were just movin' small weight 'round on the streets," Kareem voiced. "Then that first attack on our boy happened. And after that, shit went left from there."

"That's 'cause they had Jamal helpin' them," Blaze intervened. "We really just gon' have to take him down and they'll be defenseless without him. If he's the brains behind their own operation, they gon' be nothin' without him."

"Exactly," Kareem responded. "We just gotta focus on bringin' him down."

"Why do you think he agreed to start workin' wit' them in the first place?" Marq queried.

"Money," Blaze suggested. "Greed... Anika."

Blaze knew that Jamal must have realized that Anika was seeing Blaze, and working with Leek would have been the perfect opportunity to get revenge on Blaze. Taking Anika away must have just been one of those spur of the moment type plans because once they had her, they didn't seem to have a clue what to do with her. And they certainly didn't seem to know how to use her to their advantage. It had been a silly plan in the first place and benefited them in no way shape or form.

"Well now they all gon' regret comin' for us from the very start," Kareem confidently announced. "Cause when we done with them, they gon' wish they had neva been born."

"Believe that," Marquise concluded.

"Yup," Blaze agreed. "We definitely gon' finish them once and for all."

"And after we finish them, we can start workin' on how y'all gon' get yo' chicks back," Marquise declared.

"I'm tired of givin' Sadie space," Kareem said with a groan. "I miss her crazy ass."

"Lord knows I miss Anika," Blaze voiced. "All this space shit is despressin'. I'on wanna do it no more."

"Me neither," Kareem agreed.

"So what'chu wanna do niggas?" Marquise questioned them both curiously.

They both kept silent before Blaze came to a conclusion.

"I'ma go get her back today."

Kareem decided to follow suit. "Same here nigga. I'm done wit' this whole break shit. She loves me, I love her, we just gotta fix this shit."

"So y'all just gon' leave and head to Sadie's?"

Kareem and Blaze both nodded in agreement before getting out their seats.

They loved their women and they were going to fight for them.

***

Anika couldn't stop thinking about him. She missed him. She missed his voice. His touch. His laugh. His scent. Everything.

She missed the great times they shared together...

She missed their private conversations...

She missed making him annoyed only to make him happy again when they made love.

"You got anything else you wanna say?" she queried curiously, crossing her arms tighter across her chest.

Blaze quickly shook his head no. "Nothing at all?" she asked again, a look of fury starting to form on her pretty face.

"Nah," he responded sheepishly.

"Okay then, shut my door on your way out."

"Huh?"

"You heard me," she snapped. "Shut my door on your wa-"

He suddenly cut across her. "I ain't goin' anywhere Anika."

"Yes you are," she stated sternly. "You said you don't have anything else to say, then you can fucking go."

"And who the fuck do you think you cursin' at right now, Anika?" Blaze wasn't liking this newly found attitude of hers at all.

"At you, Malik!" she exclaimed, pointing at him rudely. "I'm cursing at fucking you!"

"I don't know who the fuck you talkin' to right now, 'cause it certainly ain't me Anika!" he shouted, taking small steps forward away from her door. With each step he took forward, Anika slowly stepped back. "I came here to talk to yo' rude ass, but it seems like you got me fucked up."

"You're the one that's not being clear about what you want, Malik!"

"Oh... I'm the one that's not bein' clear?" he questioned her sarcastically. "But look who's the one that wants me to fuckin' go!"

"You're engaged! To someone else that isn't me, so what the hell do you want from me, Malik?"

"You know what I wan' Anika. I told you this shit already when I had you in my crib," he said, becoming frustrated with her.

"Well it seems like you're just playing games with me," she declared.

"How the fuck am I playin' games Anika?! I told yo' ass already I want to start somethin' with you," he fumed, moving to stand in front of her.

She looked up at him, becoming slightly intimidated by the way he was towering over her and glaring down with those grey eyes. "But you're still engaged to Masika! I'm not going to be your side chi-"

"But who am I fuckin', you or Masika?"

She kept silent for a while before answering with a shrug. "You could be fucking some other chick."

"But I ain't!" he shouted, knowing deep down he was lying. But fucking Desiree was a mistake that wasn't going to happen again. He would make sure of it. "I'm only fuckin' you, because I only want to fuck you!"

"But what about Mas-"

He suddenly interrupted her. "I'm endin' shit with her, so don't worry 'bout her."

"But yo-"

"Anika, don't let me have to tell yo' ass again. I'm done with her, and anyone else. I want you, a'ight? You the only one gettin' this dick from now on, a'ight?"

Anika slowly nodded, biting her lips sexily at him. All his shouting and him going off on her had low-key turned her on. And now she wanted him.

"So stop fuckin' worryin' about shit that don't matter!" he concluded loudly before walking straight past her and heading straight for her bedroom.

Anika stayed still in her place, smiling to herself as she thought of how she was loving Blaze's dominant and cocky side towards her. She already knew that he wasn't one to mess with, but she liked messing with him.

"Get yo' sexy ass in here!" he shouted from her bedroom and she quickly obeyed, running blissfully to her bedroom. "Yes daaaddy," she sweetly sang.

Once inside, she noticed him sitting on the edge of her lilac king-sized bed and watching her seductively with those grey eyes that she loved so much.

"Get naked," he ordered firmly, still watching her carefully. He couldn't wait to get in between those tender thighs of hers and give her a good dicking down that would assure his new commitment to her.

Anika slowly untied her robe straps, pulled it off her body, letting it fall straight to the ground. She smiled sexily as Blaze's eyes widened with lust and she sauntered closer to him, until she was sitting on his lap with her legs folded against his thighs.

His hands went straight to her ass cheeks and gently rubbed on her firm flesh, before moving his head closer to the side of her neck.

"Malik..." Anika gently moaned his name as he got right to work. Rubbing on her ass and kissing her neck was rapidly driving her crazy and she wanted nothing more than to feel his thick, long length buried inside her.

Things only got more heated between them once Anika started rubbing her naked pussy on Blaze's rock hard erection, teasing him to complete hardness.

"Fuck... Anika, you know what you doin' to me right now," Blaze gently groaned in her ear, moving his big hands up her body and using his thumbs to play with her nipples.

"I want you so bad," Anika whispered, her voice drunk with lust and sex.

"Hmm... How bad you wan' me, baby?"

"So fucking bad," Anika said with a soft sigh, still grinding on his hard erection. "I want to... feel your big dick inside me... Fucking me... Making me cum all day."

She missed making him happy and keeping him well fed.

Finally making it to his kitchen, Blaze was greeted by a seductive goddess, in nothing but a pink silk robe, hands on the marble kitchen countertop, smiling happily at him.

"You're just in time," Anika greeted him warmly. "I cooked you a little something."

Anika had definitely not just cooked Blaze a little something. As his eyes began to wander, his stomach began to growl with even more hunger and anticipation for some food inside him already. On the kitchen counter in front of her, there were various dishes and bowls filled with the plentiful foods that Anika had cooked for him.

It wasn't even Thanksgiving, but with the amount of food she had prepared just for him, Blaze knew that Thanksgiving had come early.

Two hours later, after having a feast together, Blaze and Anika found themselves cuddling and chilling on his black loveseat, with a Netflix show playing on the plasma in front of them. With his arms wrapped around her and her body leaning against his, the both of them felt so in love by being in each other's arms.

"You enjoy the meal I made for you?" Anika questioned him shyly.

"Course I did," he responded. "You definitely need to do that shit more often."

"More often, Malik?" Anika's left brow rose up in surprise and a small smirk grew on her lips.

"Yeah, more often, bae," he pushed. "Like every single day."

"Uh-uh!" Anika protested sternly. "That meal took ages Blaze, and I'm still drained from standing in the kitchen all day. Besides, you can cook, right? Cook you something to eat tomorrow."

"But I want my lady cookin' for me," Blaze whispered gently, moving his soft lips to the side of her neck. "She's the only one who can throw it down in the kitchen."

"Uh-uh, I know what you're trying to do Malik, and it ain't gonna work... Mmm, Malik," Anika gently moaned at the feel of Blaze's lips kissing on her sensitive neck.

"Say you'll cook for me baby," Blaze cajoled her sweetly between his seductive kisses.

"Mmm... Uh-uh... Malik you can cook for yourself."

"I know. But I want you cookin' for me tomorrow, in nothing but yo' panties on."

MISS JENESEQUA

Anika couldn't help but fall in love with his neck kisses. And when she felt that warm tongue of his swirling on her skin, she knew she was officially a goner. "Mmmm Malik... Nothing but my panties on?"

"Absolutely nothing," he whispered sexily into her ear.

"How about we ditch the panties and I cook you breakfast in nothing but my Louboutins?" she asked sexily. "Actually, I don't even really need to cook anything. You got everything you need to eat right between my thighs. All you gotta do is get on your knees and eat this pussy."

"Damn Nika, you bad girl," Blaze stated amusingly. Her confidence was turning him on, he couldn't lie about that.

"I'm bad for you," she replied lustfully.

"Only me?" he asked, lifting her chin up so she was forced to stare up into those mesmerizing grey eyes of his that she adored so much.

"Only you, Malik."

But missing him and wanting to be with him again were two different things at the moment for Anika. She missed him, but was she willing to get back with him right now?

She knew that she loved him and she couldn't see herself with anyone else but him. Even with the problems they were going through right now, they were still engaged to be married.

Suddenly, a loud knock on Sadie's door sounded and Anika looked from where she sat on the couch to the front door.

"Sadi-"

"Already on it girl," Sadie quickly cut her off, as she walked out her kitchen towards her front door and began unlocking it. "It's probably my girl, Latisha. I told her to drop..." Sadie's words suddenly began to trail off once she realized who she had just opened the door to.

Anika's eyes widened with surprise as she watched Sadie's now open, front door.

There in all their glory stood Blaze and Kareem.

"Miss me?" Kareem cockily asked Sadie, breaking the mini silence that had brewed between them.

"Get the fuck ou-"

"We ain't goin' nowhere," Blaze stated firmly, stepping deeper into her apartment, both eyes plastered on Anika's.

With the way those mesmerizing grey eyes were now watching her, she realized how serious he was and how he was bent on talking to her. And with how fine he was looking right now, she knew she wouldn't be able to resist hearing him out.

Oh shit...

CHAPTER 20 ~ A THUG'S LOVE

Oh shit...

Why was he doing this to her?

Clad in a dark blue Ralph Lauren polo shirt, black denim jeans, black timberland boots with two silver chains and a diamond stud in each ear, Anika sure had missed admiring her man. It wasn't fair what he was doing. Rocking up to Sadie's apartment looking so damn fine, and demanding to speak to her.

Reluctantly, she agreed to head into the bedroom she was staying in and hear him out. It's not like she had a choice in the matter anyways. He was going to talk to her whether she liked it or not.

Now, here he stood by the closed door, with his muscular arms crossed and his grey eyes fixated upon hers. Even when she looked away trying to ease the tension growing between them, his eyes still stared at her not willing to let go.

"Blaze, I..."

"I fired Candi," he suddenly revealed.

"Oh..." She paused momentarily before adding, "Is that supposed to make everything better?"

"Nah," he said. "I just wanted to let you know."

"Okay."

"Stop makin' shit awkward, Nika," Blaze demanded firmly. "I'm here because I miss you and I want you back."

"But did you forget why you lost me in the first place?" she asked him curiously.

"I know I fucked up wit' Candi, but I apologize," he stated sincerely. "She doesn't mean shit to me. I know how much revenue she brings into the club but I let her go 'cause I respect and value our relationship. I'on wan' us to fight anymore, baby. I just want you back. I miss you baby... Don't you miss me?"

"I miss you..." Her words trailed off as she took a soft sigh.

"So why can't we get back togetha now ba-"

"I miss you but you drive me crazy, Malik," she revealed simply. "I'm not sure if bein' with you is healthy."

"How's it not healthy?"

"I don't know... It just drives me crazy," she explained. "I feel crazy being with you sometimes and now I'm feeling crazy not being with you."

"So stop feelin' crazy and just be wit' me," he suggested confidently. "I'm sorry for all the drama and bullshit, but I know what I wan'. And that's you, Nika. I wan' to marry you and start a family togetha."

"What about being in the game?" she asked. "You took the job offer from Sergio."

"I called him up and I declined."

"You declined?"

Blaze nodded at her, smiling. "I declined, baby. I thought 'bout what you said and I realized that you were right, I'on need this job. Not when I have you."

"So you're not accepting it?"

Blaze shook his head no at her before moving closer to her, where she sat on the edge of the bed. Anika's eyes widened with surprise as he stepped closer to her, and she found her breath quickening when he took a seat right next to her. That's how much of an effect he had on her.

"Anika... I love you and I'm sorry," he whispered into her ear sweetly. "Say you forgive me girl... I miss you so much."

As soon as he reached for her hand, Anika swore she felt a strong wave of electricity flow through her. Feeling his hand hold onto hers, had her currently feeling all types of strong emotions. But she knew one thing for sure, she loved this man and no matter what they had or were going through, she wanted to spend the rest of her life with him.

"I forgive you, Malik," she whispered back to him.

He looked down at her as he lifted her chin up, so she was forced to stare directly into his grey eyes. Those grey eyes that she had fallen so deeply and utterly in love with.

"What'chu say?" he happily queried.

"I forgive you and I love you Malik," she repeated only adding to Blaze's delight.

"Say it again," he pushed cockily, his grey eyes lighting up like diamonds.

Anika chuckled lightly before repeating her words again. "I forgive you and I love you Malik."

"I love you too, baby," he responded lovingly before adding, "I promise I won't ever make you cry again... Unless it's in the bedroom 'cause I'm murderin' that bomb ass pussy."

Anika lightly hit him on his chest before replying, "You such a freak Malik."

"And that's why yo' ass gon' foreva love me, right?"

She grinned happily then spoke, "Right."

Blaze then branded his lips down to hers so they could kiss passionately after being away from each other for so long. He sure had missed her and he was glad to know that they had sorted things out.

"No more secrets Malik."

"No more secrets baby," he repeated after her.

"We need to communicate more and you need to understand that I'm not with you because of how much money you have or what you give me, I'm with you because I love you."

"I hear ya' babe."

"I know that being in the game is your job but I want you to leave one day. Not now, but soon."

"I know babe, and when you ask, I swear I'm gon' be ready to carry out yo' wish," he informed her gently.

Anika was just glad that they were moving on to better things. They had finally stopped arguing and managed to come to a mutual understanding in their relationship. The only thing that they needed to do from here on out was work on their communication together and start planning their wedding together.

"When do you wan' start plannin' the weddin', bae?" Blaze questioned her curiously, holding her waist as she sat on his lap.

"As soon as possible," she said calmly. "I wasn't feeling up to it before but I really want to start planning now."

"That's good, baby," he stated coolly. "You know I can't wait to take yo' sexy ass down the aisle."

"And I can't wait to officially be your Mrs. King," Anika concluded before locking her lips onto his again, to steal another passionate kiss from him.

After a few more minutes of kissing, Anika decided that she wanted to go back home with Blaze. He quickly helped her pack her shit up and before she knew it, she was shouting goodbye out to Sadie who was still in her bedroom talking to Kareem.

"Sadie, I'm leavin' with Blaze, I'll call you later tonight!"

"Alright girl, don't forget girl! Bye!"

Then Anika was quick out the door, holding Blaze's hand as they both headed to his Ferrari downstairs.

Sadie sighed softly as she heard her front door suddenly close. She knew that Blaze and Anika were going to be just fine and were going to sort out their issues with no problems. As for her and this fool? She wasn't so sure.

"Sadie, please talk to me."

Sadie looked down at her carpeted floor, not wanting to spend another second staring at his handsome face.

Damn, she had missed him.

Missed him more than she realized. And seeing him in her apartment looking so attractive still, after all their time apart, only made her angry. Why'd he still have to be so fine?

She wasn't sure what she wanted. She knew that she missed him. She loved him. But he had hurt her and honestly the heartbreak from that alone had been too much to bear.

"How many times do I have to keep on fuckin' apologizing to you for you to understand that I regret what happened, and if I could take the shit back I would?" he retorted, getting frustrated with what she was doing.

Sadie's head snapped up only so she could look at this nigga while he talked to her. The tone in his voice was one that she wasn't liking. He had no right to be angry as far as she was concerned. If anyone should have been angry, it should have been her alone.

"Firstly, I'm not likin' the attitude I'm hearin' in yo' damn voice nigga," she snapped. "Cut that shit out."

"Well talkin' gently to you doesn't fuckin' work no more," he spat. "Cause you don't fuckin' listen."

"Well, maybe you should go and talk gently to your new bitch, Satin."

"You know I don't want Satin! I want yo' ass!" he shouted at her.

"That's not what it looked like when I found you kissing her," Sadie fumed.

"She seduced me, Sadie," he reminded her. "I didn't want her at all. I just want you. I've divorced her 'cause I want to be wit' you."

"You should have told me you were married from the start," Sadie said. "I didn't want to find out from that bitch."

"I apologize for not tellin' you baby, but it wasn't intentional," he gently explained. "Truth was, I was scared."

"And why were you scared nigga?"

"Cause of how you would react," he stated simply. "I didn't want you to start overreactin', thinkin' I was cheatin' on you or somethin'."

"You should have just told me."

"I know, bae," he answered, slowly moving from where he stood near her door and moving towards where she sat on her bed. Then he got down on his knees in front of her. "But I'm sorry and I swear I won't keep shit away from you again."

"I just don't know if I can trust you again, 'Reem," she declared sadly. "I don't know if we're meant to-"

"We were made for each other," he commented, cutting her off. "I made one silly mistake but I swear I'm not gon' make any more mistakes. I love you so much, Sadie, and I really wan' spend the rest of my life wit' you."

"You've got to earn my trust back," she ordered sternly.

"I swear I will bae."

"You've got to show me how much you love me every day."

"I will baby."

"You've got to treat me like the Queen I truly am, every single day," she demanded with a devilish smile.

All Kareem could do was smile and nod, promising to do whatever she asked. All he wanted to do was make her happy. That's all he ever wanted to do.

"Alright... I forgive you 'Ree-"

Sadie didn't even get a chance to finish her sentence because before she knew it, Kareem's thick lips were sealed on hers and he was lifting her up so that he could place her in the center of her pink king-sized California bed.

"Mmmm..." She moaned as he kissed her, already starting to build her burning desire for him after all the time they had been apart. Once she was comfortably in the center of her bed, ready for things to get even more heated, Kareem suddenly pulled away from the kiss.

"Baby, I love you so much and I'm sorry for all the shit that went down."

Sadie nodded at him, bringing one of her hands up to stroke his left cheek. "And you know that you the woman I want to spend the rest of my life with. I fell in love with you the first moment I laid eyes on you. I can't imagine livin' even another second without you. I want to continue to share every moment of my life with you, I will always take care of you and give you my full support, no matter what bae."

She couldn't stop smiling and by the look in Kareem's eyes, she could sense that he was trying to tell her something. Something very important.

At first, she immediately thought he was proposing. She was expecting a ring to pop out from somewhere, but it never came. What came instead was a gentle kiss on her forehead and a second "I love you."

Sadie couldn't lie and say that she wasn't disappointed because she was. She was very disappointed, but all that really mattered was that they had sorted shit out between them finally.

However, right now, Sadie wasn't in the mood to make love anymore. What she really wanted to do was head to her kitchen to prepare a meal for herself and her man. She slowly pulled her body away from under Kareem's and took this opportunity to get off the bed. It would be nice for them to have a nice reunion meal.

"Is somethin' wrong sweetheart?" he questioned her curiously.

"No babe, I'm just gonna make us something to eat real quick," she sweetly answered before leaving the room.

As she made her way towards her kitchen, Sadie realized that she wanted to get married to Kareem sooner than later. It seemed like the perfect time for him to propose, but she understood why he hadn't. He probably wasn't prepared yet. And because of that, Sadie knew she would just have to be patient and wait.

As she began to fumble for pots and pans in her kitchen, she was quickly disturbed as the doorbell rang.

Sadie groaned momentarily, not wanting to see anyone at this time. She just wanted to be alone for a bit as she prepared her meal for her and her man.

However, she slowly left her kitchen and walked to her front door and opened it. She was expecting to see someone standing right in front of her, but no one stood. Although once she looked down at the floor, she saw the cutest thing ever.

A small black Bombay kitten, with blue eyes and small cute pointed ears sat on a small red velvet cushion.

She couldn't help but crouch down low to stroke it. Her love for kittens had stemmed from her childhood because she always had found them so adorable.

"Hello cutie... What's this?" Sadie suddenly noticed the kitten's red heart collar and saw that it said her name.

She turned it around and saw in bold, italic gold writing:

"Baby, will you marry me?"

CHAPTER 21 ~ HIS BABY GIRL

Sadie immediately gasped, unable to hide her shock and excitement. She wanted him to propose but since he hadn't done it earlier, she figured she would just have to wait. But now he had organized this whole thing. He knew how much she loved cats and he had thoughtfully thought of a way to incorporate that into his proposal.

"Well will you?" Kareem's deep, sexy baritone spoke from behind her.

As soon as he had decided with Blaze that they were going to get their ladies back today, he just knew that proposing to his baby was happening today. He had planned it for weeks and now that it was finally here, he couldn't lie and say he wasn't nervous.

She turned around to see him on one knee and holding up an opened black ring box. She got up from her knees and walked up to him, with a huge smile plastered upon her pretty face and tears wanting to fall.

The ring alone made her want to scream. Scream out to the whole Atlanta and show them all how beautiful her engagement ring was. The very expensive looking white gold diamond ring finally made the tears burst out of her eyes.

"I love you so much. When I first met you I could not have imagined what our relationship would grow into, or how much yo' ass would mean to me, although from the second I met yo' crazy ass I knew that you were very special. Now I know how very special you really are, and I'm so in love with you baby girl. You've taken me to a place that I couldn't have believed possible. Let's continue this foreva, buildin' the perfect life, and growin' old togetha. I'ma be yo' knight in shining armor, yo' king there to protect you from all that life can throw at you. Be my wife, and give me the privilege of bein' your husband, always and foreva Sadie."

He took her hand and looked nervously into her eyes. "Sadie Maiya Clark, will you marry me?"

How could she say no to this fine man who she absolutely loved and adored? Sure they had been through their ups and downs, but what couple hadn't? He meant everything to her and this is all she wanted. They had moved pretty fast during the past few months, but fuck it. This is what she wanted and she knew that this was what he wanted too.

"Yes Mr. Kareem Tyler Smith, I will marry you!"

He quickly slid the beautiful ring on her ring finger before getting up, gently lifting her up in the air and passionately kissing her. Their tongues had already begun to battle, dance and sing a tune that was growing sweeter by the second.

She was going to be his wife and he was so damn happy! He thanked God that she had agreed and said yes because if for some reason she had decided to say no and decline his request, he would have been devastated.

Sadie slowly pulled away from his lips. "Baby, I love you and I'm so excited to be your wife." The love and excitement in Kareem's eyes were undeniable.

"Darlin', you already know how much I love yo' ass and I can't wait to see you in yo' pretty white dress." Kareem then tried to latch his lips back onto hers, but she turned her face to the side so that he ended up kissing her cheek.

"What about the kitten?" Sadie questioned him, wondering if it was still there or not.

"Nah babe, it's gone." He turned her around so that she could look and see that the kitten was no longer there. While he was on one knee in front of her, the owner of the kitten had discretely given him a thumbs up and taken it away. "I knew you would want to keep it, but you know we can't bae." He rested his chin on her shoulder and wrapped his arms around her waist.

"Hmm, I know. You're allergic."

"Exactly." He began to kiss the side of her neck. "But you know what I ain't allergic to?"

"What baby?" Sadie couldn't help but sexily bite her lips as his sweet kisses progressed up her neck.

"You."

Five minutes later, Sadie was on her kitchen counter and 'Reem was deep in between her legs, making her speak a language only he could understand.

BAD FOR MY THUG 3: THE FINALE

"Shit! Baby! Uhhh... Yassssss, just... just like that... Fuck!"

Her handsome, freaky fiancé definitely knew how to treat her pussy right and she was truly happy with knowing that he was hers forever.

No one else's.

***

Anika and Malik didn't even make it past the front door before they jumped on one another. They couldn't help it. They had missed each other so much.

But after composing themselves and finally making it to their bedroom, shit got heated pretty quickly.

Blaze wanted to taste his baby so bad. He was feeling hungry but not for food, for her alone.

He looked up into her beautiful brown eyes and got down on his knees, unable to wait any longer. He gently separated her thighs apart, burying his face in the heavenly valley between her thighs. He slipped his hand between her legs, dipping his fingers between her wet lips. She was so hot and tight for him.

Gently parting her lips with his thumbs, Blaze slowly rolled his tongue over Anika's clit, tasting her honey-sweet arousal. Her hands gently clenched to his freshly, waved hair, watching his face dive into her wet pussy. Then he decided to pull back and be a tease for a little bit.

"Uhhhh," Anika moaned loudly as Blaze ran his thick index finger between her damp lips, sending a cold shiver down her exposed back.

"Pussy so wet for me bae," he whispered seductively before parting her wet lips, leaning his face in and pressing his tongue flat against her wet flesh. Another moan escaped free from her lips, as Blaze flicked his long tongue against her soaked folds, then pushed into her tightness, fucking her slowly with as much of his length as he could fit.

His grey eyes locked onto hers and Anika immediately whimpered for more. His thumb pressed firmly to her clit, nudging it back and forth as his tongue wriggled between her tight walls.

Blaze groaned against her wetness, only making Anika moan louder. His tongue pushed in and out of her pussy more rapidly, and she couldn't help herself now. She began grinding against his face, grabbed his freshly trimmed head and pushed his head down further between her legs.

He groaned into her, licked and sucked her tender flesh. Anika's sweet juices now began to gloss his lips, tongue and chin. He decided to ease two fingers into her tight hole, only to drive her crazy even further and it worked.

Anika's thighs began to shake, as Blaze's talented tongue continued to swirl and lick, she could feel the hot pressure building deep within her. All he was doing was just driving her crazier and crazier and crazier by the second. When it came to eating her out, he always knew the right shit to do. He then reached up with his free hand, and squeezed her left breast in his big, warm palm.

"Uhh... Shit, baby don't stop...please don't stooop," she exhaled shakily, grasping his head tight, arching her back off the edge of the bed. "Agh! Uhh, fuuck!"

Blaze was really making her feel good, and she didn't like it one bit. She loved it.

Blaze's wet tongue lashed up against Anika's swollen clit and he commanded her with his sexy, deep, husky voice.

"Cum baby."

Anika whimpered and her head fell back. Her walls clenched tightly around his probing fingers and tongue. Then before she knew it, her whole entire body began to shake and she came for him, bathing his slick mouth with her precious, sweet nectar.

He lapped up every drop, pressing his nose against her clit, inhaling her deeply. Her body shivered, and she watched him kiss her warm inner thighs softly.

"You taste fuckin' delicious girl," he said seductively, licking up all her remaining juices from his thick fingers.

Anika sighed deeply one last time, watching as Blaze climbed on top of her, positioning his hard dick right between her thighs.

"I swear Daddy gon' dick you down real good," he whispered to her, gently stroking her thighs and slowly entering inside her. "All night tonight baby girl."

***

BAD FOR MY THUG 3: THE FINALE

Marquise sighed deeply as he reminisced on all that had gone down in just a matter of eight months. Blaze had met Anika, Kareem and Sadie had finally hooked up, and he had met Naomi. He knew how much he loved Naomi and wanted to spend the rest of his life with her. He just wished that her husband would learn to leave her the fuck alone and understand that their marriage was over.

In just a matter of eight months, The Lyons had foolishly tried to come for the Knight Nation and only continued to fail. Yeah, they had attacked their turfs a few times, managed to take Anika, and blown up their entire warehouse, but those were all petty, low blows. Compared to what the Knight Nation could really do, The Lyons' acts so far had all been child's play.

If it wasn't for Blaze's promise to Anika about not killing Jamal, then Marquise was sure that Blaze wouldn't have hesitated in spending an entire day hunting him down and murdering him. But Marquise understood that Blaze's promise to Anika was more important to him than just getting revenge. Shit was changing because of who they were all in love with, and Marq knew that things were only changing for the good.

Just as Marquise decided to leave the new main warehouse, he heard the sudden bang of metal against the entrance door downstairs.

He knew he was the only one about, so if trouble was around, he would have to be strong enough to defend himself.

He immediately lifted the back of his red shirt, only to reach for the blue .9mm hiding in the waistband of his jeans.

Once the metal banging had stopped, Marquise kept still and listened carefully for the sound of movement, coming up the stairs to the second floor where he was. But he seemed to hear none.

Slowly, he crept out the room he was in. Quickly he looked left and right down the wooden corridors, each attached with a long staircase leading downstairs. It was when he stepped completely out the room that the first bullet came flying.

Bang!

Marquise quickly ducked, trying to take cover but also wanting to see the person who was starting trouble with him tonight. But he could already sense it was Leek or one of those other fools at their squad. It couldn't be Jamal though. One thing the boys had noticed about Jamal was that he never liked doing dirty work himself, he preferred someone doing it for him.

Bang! Bang! Bang!

Marquise couldn't take it anymore. He needed to know because if it ended up being Leek, then he wouldn't hesitate in sending a single bullet through his head.

Marquise jumped up, gun in hand and looked over the balcony to see who was on the ground floor shooting bullets up at him.

The minute his eyes locked onto Leek's determined ones, Marquise didn't hesitate in cocking his gun back and gunning straight for him.

If he had to be the one to end this fool tonight, then so be it.

CHAPTER 22 ~ ONE SHOT ONE KILL

"Look at chu..."

Anika blushed, her light skin flaring up pink as Blaze stared lovingly at her, with his strong, muscular arms wrapped around her slim waist. She loved the sound of his deep voice in the mornings. It had a raspy undertone within it and it turned her on in ways that made her want to have all his babies.

"Look at chu though..."

Anika couldn't help but shyly smile with the way Blaze was holding onto her while he lay behind her. His fresh, warm breath tickled her neck and she giggled slightly at how good and ticklish it felt.

"You so sexy, bae," he complimented her seductively. "Just look at how fuckin' sexy yo' ass is."

"Blaze stoppp," Anika laughingly stated, still blushing at his compliments and the way he was looking at her.

"Stop what?" he asked her. "Don't front like you ain't know it's true. You know how fuckin' bad and sexy you are girl."

"Thank you baby," she thanked him happily, turning around to face him.

"No problem bae."

As soon as they had gotten back home yesterday, they couldn't keep their hands off each other. Now waking up, they still couldn't stop. It was only 10am but Blaze and Anika had already added two rounds to their numerous rounds from last night.

From the look in her lust filled eyes, Blaze knew that his little freak was definitely craving him some more.

"Damn Nika," he voiced gently. "Yo' freaky ass neva gets tired, huh?"

She shook her head no, licking her lips at him sexually before leaning closer to the side of his neck and beginning to kiss on his soft, warm skin.

"Hmm, that feels good bae," he whispered, quietly groaning at her moves to make him feel good.

Just as things were getting heated between them, Blaze's iPhone immediately started ringing.

"I just fucked yo' bitch in some Gucci flip-flops..."

Blaze annoyingly groaned at the ringing, getting angry at someone interrupting his quality time with his wifey.

"Ignore it baby," Anika instructed him as she continued to pleasure him with her seductive neck kisses.

But as the phone continued to ring, Blaze could sense it was important. He didn't know what it was, but he just felt like if he didn't pick up the phone, he would regret it later.

"Let me just answer it real quick beautiful," he cajoled Anika sweetly. "Promise you gon' have me all to yo'self again."

Anika sighed deeply but nodded reluctantly, and let him reach for his phone lying on the lampstand opposite him. He picked up his smartphone and answered his incoming call.

"Sup?"

Anika placed one hand on his hard chest, softly rubbing her warm hand over it, as she patiently waited for him to get off the phone.

However, seeing the way his grey eyes suddenly began to widen with anger and shock, she just knew that their quality time for today was over.

"What hospital?"

Anika's worry grew with hearing the word hospital. From the sound of things, it seemed like someone was hurt.

"I'm on my way," Blaze confirmed before ending the call.

"What is it Malik?" Anika gently asked him, concerned about what was going on.

"Marquise's been shot," he stated.

"What?! Is he okay?"

"He's... decent. Just restin' right now, but I think he's good."

"Okay... Do you know who shot him?"

BAD FOR MY THUG 3: THE FINALE

"Leek," he revealed plainly. "Leek shot him just before Marq killed him."

"Oh wow... Can I come with you to go to see Marq?"

Blaze nodded at her before responding, "Yeah bae. Let's start gettin' ready to go."

Half an hour later, Anika and Blaze were walking hand in hand, down the hospital ward corridor leading to Marquise's room.

When finding it, they entered only to be greeted by Kareem, Sadie, a wide awake Marquise, and a female near his side that Anika was sure she had never seen before.

"B', you finally made it," Marquise greeted him with a smirk.

"Hell yeah I made it," Blaze said with a frown, leaving Anika's side so that he could move closer to Marquise's bedside. "You almost gave me a fuckin' heart attack, nigga. You a'ight tho?"

"Yeah, I'm straight," Marquise responded simply. "If it weren't for my Queen right here comin' to my rescue when I called..." He turned to look up at the unknown female that had yet to be introduced to Blaze and Anika, with a sexy smile. "Lord knows I wouldn't have a leg no fuckin' more."

"That's where the bullet hit?" Kareem queried curiously, only to receive a head nod from Marquise.

"Wait, wait hold up... This is Nicol... I mean Naomi?" Blaze asked, looking from Marquise to the female right by his side.

Anika began to inspect her up and down, admiring her gorgeous facial features and how good she looked next to Marq. She was caramel, with long straight brown hair that went past her hips, and gorgeous honey brown eyes.

"Yup," Marquise replied. "This is Naomi y'all, my girlfriend."

Naomi shyly smiled at them and gave them all a little wave.

"Nah, fuck all that wavin' shit, don't be shy bae," Marquise announced boldly, staring at her seriously as he reached for her hand. "This my family. You gotta be comfortable with them."

"I'm not shy, Marq," she voiced softly with a small smile. "Hey guys."

"Hey, nice to meet you," Anika greeted her warmly. "I'm Anika, Blaze's fiancé."

"It's good to finally know that Marquise's girlfriend ain't imaginary," Blaze declared amusingly, only to get a light hit from Anika on his chest. "Nice to finally meet you though ma', I'm Bl-"

"Blaze," Naomi said, cutting him off. "Marq's told me so much about you. And Kareem."

"Don't believe everythin' that nigga tells you 'bout us," Kareem informed her. "Especially the bad shit."

Naomi lightly chuckled before turning to Sadie. "And you must be Kareem's girl... Sadie, right?"

"The one and only," Sadie responded with a large grin. "I'm his fiancée too."

"Bitch, what?!" Anika suddenly shrieked, running to Sadie frantically. "He proposed?"

Sadie quickly flashed Anika her left hand and they both started screaming and jumping happily at the diamond ring on her finger.

"Congrats nigga," Blaze stated with a pleased facial expression. "Bout fuckin' time."

"Yeah, congrats fool, but stop tryna steal the spotlight," Marquise joked. "I gotta tell you niggas 'bout the shootin'."

"A'ight, we listenin'," 'Reem responded.

Marquise explained how he was alone at the warehouse, and suddenly heard a loud banging of metal at the front door. He kept silent for a while, heard nothing and decided to check the premises. It was then that he heard gunshots and when he finally got a chance to look at who was shooting, he saw Leek's face and aimed straight for the kill.

"One shot, one kill," Marquise stated. "One bullet to the head and he was finally down. I didn't realize I was shot until I started movin' again, so I knew I had to call for help. The only person I wanted next to me was Naomi, so I called her. I know I probably should have called y'all niggas, but y'all had just gotten back wit' yo' girls and shit, I didn't wan' to kill yo' moments yet. So Naomi came to get me, then I got here, they took the bullet out and now I'm straight."

"Well, you ain't exactly straight with that damn cast wrapped around yo' leg," Blaze pointed out.

"Yeah, but I'm alive and that's all that really matters," Marquise answered. "As for Jamal, y'all are just gon' have to find him without me and finish the plan."

Blaze and Kareem nodded at him firmly, knowing that for this to be truly finished, Jamal had to be sorted.

"Baby…"

Malik turned to his baby's gentle voice wanting to know what was up. He looked at her lovingly, waiting for her to continue to speak to him.

"Don't forget your promise," Anika reminded him seriously.

He nodded at her, trying to reassure her before speaking. "I promise I ain't gon' break it, sweetheart."

***

The war had arrived and he was going to have to face it alone.

Leek was dead and with The Lyons' leader gone, Jamal was left with only a short amount of men. All the others had left, claiming that they were loyal to Leek and Leek alone.

Now that Leek was dead, the Lyons' were finished. They didn't care about Jamal and he knew it now, too. They had only been following Leek's orders because Leek was the one who had decided to bring him into the squad. But it seemed they had never trusted him from the start. Even though he provided them with so much and helped them accomplish so much, they still hadn't trusted him.

Jamal knew that he had to be ready to defend himself, because it was clear that these stupid ass niggas weren't going to do it for him.

He had to be ready to deal with Blaze because he knew that he was coming.

And when he came, Jamal would be ready.

Ready for war.

CHAPTER 23 ~ HUNT

"A'ight so I'ma call the boys to check his office, his usual chilling spots 'round Atlanta and his crib, even though he hasn't been there for a few days now," Kareem explained.

"Yeah, they already been watchin' those spots," Blaze said calmly. "No harm in lookin' again, though."

"I think we should go check out his office though, and wherever else we may think he may be at right now," Kareem suggested.

"Yeah, actually, that don't sound half bad. Let's do it."

Kareem and Blaze got into Blaze's Ferrari and while Blaze drove them to their various destinations, Kareem stayed alert, looking at his phone, waiting for any contact from one of their soldiers, notifying them on Jamal's whereabouts.

"I'ma be so glad when this shit is all ova," Kareem announced with a deep sigh. "We all been thru so much shit 'cause of this guy and his fuckin' games."

"I know, right," Blaze stated in agreement, his eyes still focused on the road ahead of him. "I swear it's like he was sent from the devil to come and knock us down."

"And he almost managed too," Kareem pointed out. "If it wasn't for how strong we are as a unit and as brothers, they would have torn us apart."

"True, true," Blaze replied with stiff head nod. "I'm just glad it's all gon' be ova. I just wan' focus on my relationship with Anika right now and with this weddin' comin' up, I know it'll only be a matter of time before Nika gets pregnant again."

"Damn, y'all really been goin' at it, huh?" Kareem asked with a hearty chuckle.

"Yeah man," Blaze responded with a smirk. "What can I say, she's addicted to me."

"Yeah not gon' lie, Sadie been all up on me too. It's like that break just made everythin' so much better. Communication been great. Sex been fuckin' amazin' and now that I've proposed, she's always so damn happy."

"Yup, it's all been somethin'," Blaze declared. "In a way, this whole situation has been not only a curse but a blessin' too. Just look at all the shit that's happened while it's all been goin' on."

"Yeah, I guess you right nigga... We just gotta take it as a lesson and keep it movin', focus on the future."

When arriving at Jamal's office, both Kareem and Blaze left the car to search for Jamal. But unfortunately, they didn't find him. So they decided to hit up some local spots he was usually seen at, being a popular attorney meant that he had to keep up a good appearance in the city, but now that he had involved himself with The Lyons, he seemed to have abandoned all his duties.

"This nigga really makin' us play cat and mouse games with him," Kareem retorted, getting pissed that they hadn't been able to find him yet. "Where the fuck is he at?"

Blaze contemplated to himself for a while. Where could Jamal Coleman currently be? If he knew that they were coming for him, then he must have figured that they would know where he would be. It would be the place of the final showdown. The final confrontation. The final battle.

It took a minute to hit Blaze, but he finally got it after deep, quick contemplation.

"North Druid Hills," Blaze announced firmly.

"What?"

"That's where he's at," Blaze stated. "I'm sure of it."

"Where in North Druid Hills though? We already blew up their buildin'," Kareem reminded Blaze with a frown, not sure that he would be right.

"Remember the underground shed a few feet under it?" Blaze questioned him, trying to re-jog his memory of the night they went to look for Anika.

"Yeah, yeah," Kareem quickly nodded before realizing. "Oh yeah, yeah the shed! The Bulls' old secret stash spot, you think that's where the nigga at?"

MISS JENESEQUA

Blaze looked at him with a certain look before answering, "I know that's where the nigga's at. Call up the attorney, we finishin' this nigga tonight."

CHAPTER 24 ~ FINALE

Blaze and Kareem slowly left the car, and walked side by side as they headed to the damaged warehouse. Once arriving, they examined their surroundings to make sure no one was watching them, as they both crept around the damage and rubble, making their way to what used to be the back entrance.

"It's down here," Kareem informed Blaze, pointing to the brick square on the floor in front of them.

"A'ight, let's do this," Blaze decided, crouching down onto his knees so that they could both lift the roof square open and enter inside the underground shed.

When they had managed to lift it open, both of them peered inside the hole only to see complete darkness.

Blaze jumped in first, only to find the hole to be quite shallow. His head was so extremely close to hitting the roof that he had to duck. Kareem quickly followed, switching on his iPhone flashlight as a way for them to see.

"It's probably filled with tunnels," Kareem explained. "We should go-"

"I think you should stay behind, 'Reem," Blaze suggested, cutting him off.

"What? Why?"

"This is somethin' that I gotta do alone," Blaze stated. "The minute he took Nika, this shit became personal between us. It's somethin' that's gotta be finished between us."

Kareem nodded, understanding his best friend's words; he wasn't completely sure about letting him go all alone though.

"I'on wan' you to go through it all by yo'self nigga," Kareem said with a frown. "We brothers, we supposed to stick togetha."

"And we always will," Blaze reassured him. "But for now, this is somethin' I gotta do on my own, 'Reem. I just need you to stay up here and wait for the attorney to show up. If I'm not up by the time he shows up, then you know what you need to do."

It took 'Reem a minute to be okay with the idea, but he finally agreed. He understood how hurt Blaze had been the most because of Jamal, and he knew that his brother had to do this for him.

"A'ight, I got chu nigga. Be safe, fool. You got all yo' shit, right?"

Blaze nodded quickly, patting himself down to show Kareem the hard ammo he had stocked up underneath his clothing. He didn't want his brother to worry about him. He was prepared and ready for anything to go left. He was ready for the war.

So Blaze gave Kareem a boost up out the hole before heading on his own through the underground shed. He had his phone flash light on as he slowly walked through, being mindful of where he was and knowing that each step deeper only took him one step closer to trouble.

He knew that for Anika's sake, he had to make it out of there alive. He couldn't die knowing that Anika was going to be left in the world without him. She was everything to him.

Blaze walked deeper and cautiously, hoping to reach an endpoint to his destination soon. It wasn't until five minutes later when he suddenly reached a two-way tunnel. One tunnel led to more darkness whereas the other one led into some type of light. And Blaze was sure that he could hear the voices of people talking.

He decided to walk into the tunnel leading to the light and the talking voices. If he was suddenly ambushed, then all he could do was hope for the very best and pray that God was on his side as he fought back.

Blaze pulled out his silver pistol from the waistband of his jeans, and held it tightly in his hands as he walked forward into the light.

When entering the light, he was faced with what seemed like a mini man cave and in the corner of the cave, was a TV switched on and playing. In front of the TV he sat, taking a large gulp from his beer before placing it on the floor next to his feet.

Blaze's grip on his silver pistol tightened as he watched the man that he had been so anxious to find all these past few months. The man he had been so anxious to kill.

Jamal Coleman.

"Took you a minute to find me," Jamal suddenly spoke, locking eyes with Blaze. He smiled devilishly before continuing. "I see you're alone. So am I."

"You only alone 'cause those niggas realized you ain't shit and you could neva do anythin' for them but cause problems," Blaze snapped, pointing his silver pistol directly at Jamal as he sat on a plastic chair.

"I didn't cause them problems," Jamal stated. "I only gave those niggas power. Too much power in fact, that they ain't even know what the fuck to do with it all."

"It was all bullshit," Blaze spat. "Every single bit of it was all bullshit. You just ignited our beef for no damn reason."

"No, not for no reason," Jamal responded with a grin. "I certainly had my reasons. Helping the Lyons meant extra money for me and a chance for me to get my revenge on you."

"And why the fuck did you wan' get revenge on me in the first place?" Blaze rudely questioned him, watching him carefully. "I didn't do shit to you."

"Oh, but you did," Jamal explained. "You stole her away from me. She loved me, worshipped the fuckin' ground I walked on, and you came and ruined everythin'. I had to get you back, I had to make sure that you understood to not fuck with what belonged to me."

"She neva loved you."

"She did," Jamal sternly pushed. "I just neva loved her. I just loved the power I had over her, that was the best part."

Staring into his cold, unremorseful eyes had Blaze wanting to send one bullet straight through him. He wanted to end this fool and make him suffer for all the shit he had put Anika through. He had used her, raped her and taken her away from him. One single bullet would finish him completely and he wouldn't be a problem anymore.

But he promised Anika there wouldn't be any more blood. He was going to do things the right way.

"You don't fuck with me. I'm fuckin' Jamal Coleman!" he proudly shouted. "Nobody messes with me. You thought that beatin' me up that night in my office was going to scare me off, but it only made me come back harder and stronger. I had to make you pay."

"You just a crazy ass nigga who's let his power as a basic ass attorney go to his damn head. You did all this shit, only to lose. Look at you now nigga, you scared!" Blaze exclaimed, sniggering at him. "You wanted to make me pay, but look what's ended up happenin', you the only one payin' for yo' shit right now. The Lyons have deserted you and yo' credibility in this town is completely tarnished."

"No, but I've still won," Jamal announced boldly. "I'm the one that's able to go back to my status as one of the most respected attorneys and build an entire case against you, yo' drug trafficking operation and make sure you end up in jail."

Blaze looked at him, astonished at all he was saying. Did he really still believe in his sick little head that he had won this battle?

"And you stand here, pointin' a damn gun at me but I know for a fact that you can't kill me 'cause you too scared knowing you gon' get caught."

"And how the fuck would I get caught?" Blaze angrily asked through clenched teeth.

"I've told a few people if they don't suddenly hear from me for a few days, then they should start digging into you. People will come lookin' for you, start sniffin', and once they start sniffin', they won't stop and it'll only be a matter of months before they sniff you out and bam! You're in jail," Jamal said with a look of excitement and happiness at Blaze's anger. "So just admit it Blaze, I've won, not you."

"See, that's where you keep fuckin' up and bein' wrong," Blaze commented. "You claim to be one of the best, respected attorneys here, but all that shit is a lie."

"How is it a lie? I am amazing at m-"

"I know 'bout the bribin' to win cases you been doin' over the years. I also know 'bout you hidin' money from law firms you invested in and profitin' money for yo'self."

Jamal's eyes immediately widened with shock.

"You liar, you don't know shi-"

"Trust me, I know," Blaze assured him with a happy smirk. "I know so much that my attorney's given all the information to the police, includin' the location of where we are at now, and it's only a matter of time before they get here and come arrest yo' stupid ass."

Marquise's plan was completely foolproof. The day he had thought of getting the attorney Jayceon had provided Blaze, to do some sniffing, it had all proven to be worth it. Jamal was a criminal, hiding a decade worth of secrets and lies.

"You're lying, there's no wa-"

"Cayman Islands sound familiar?"

Jamal suddenly froze with fear.

"Yeah, I know all 'bout yo' storin' of fake money accounts out there," Blaze informed him simply. "You a fraudster and you always have been."

Blaze slowly lowered his gun as he watched Jamal's head begin to fall with defeat and embarrassment.

"See, I woulda killed yo' ass the minute I stepped in here," Blaze began. "But I made a promise to Anika that I wouldn't kill you. The only reason why you're alive right now is 'cause of her. That's it. Because I swear to God all I wan' do right now is make you pay for all the foul shit you did and send you to the hell yo' ass belongs in."

Jamal didn't bother to reply to any of Blaze's words. He just kept silent and Blaze was forced to watch him as he gloated in his defeat. He was just happy that this crazy, deluded and power crazed man had finally been knocked off his high horse. It was time for him to face the reality of knowing that he had lost. It was over now.

"Yo' ass made the biggest mistake of joinin' The Lyons. You shouldn't have come for me, especially since I ain't send for you. You fucked up and now you gon' pay for the consequences of what happens when you mess wit' me."

The sirens of cops from upstairs, outside, immediately began to sound, only getting closer and closer with each second.

Blaze decided that it was time for him to bounce. He had confronted Jamal and stuck to his promise to Anika. He wasn't going to kill Jamal. But he was going to make sure that he paid, by rotting in jail for the rest of his life.

He took one last glance at Jamal whose head was still bent low in deep defeat before turning on his heels out the cave.

"I may have lost the battle…" Jamal suddenly spoke out.

Blaze slowly turned around with a sigh, only to see Jamal staring at him bravely. "But only one man gets to win this war," Jamal fumed. Before Blaze could even react, Jamal lifted a black pistol out of nowhere. He instantly pointed it directly towards Blaze, cocking his gun back as he quickly aimed straight for his target. "And it's me."

Pow! Pow! Pow!

EPILOGUE ~ REIGNING KINGS

~ 6 Months Later ~

After all the shit they had been through…

After all the arguments, the drama, the near death experiences…

Blaze was happy that they were finally here, in the moment with all their family and friends around.

Auntie Ari's barbeque was in full swing, as everyone was either dancing, eating or lining up to get some food, or either laughing and cracking jokes together.

Blaze was happy to be surrounded by love and positivity right now. After the start of the year being filled with negativity and hate, he was loving the love right now.

He glanced to the left only to see Sadie sitting on 'Reem's lap, as she fed him some food off her plate. He sure was glad to see them two back together and knowing that they were getting married next month, was amazing. Despite the shit they had been through with Satin, they were stronger than ever before.

Blaze then glanced to his right only to see Marquise and Naomi sitting next to each other, with his arms on her shoulders pulling her in closer to him. They were conversing and laughing together, looking very happy as a couple. Naomi was still working on her divorce from her husband, but she had already made her decision, regardless of what some piece of paper said. She wanted Marq and for that, Blaze was happy that she was choosing the right man.

"Baby… You good?"

Was he good?

Six months ago, Jamal Coleman had almost managed to kill him. If it wasn't for the fact that Jamal hadn't realized that he had an empty gun, then Blaze wasn't sure what would have happened that day. He wasn't scared, but the whole fact that Jamal had managed to pop a gun out of nowhere, took Blaze completely off guard. Nonetheless, seeing the pale face of Coleman when he realized nothing had been fired was priceless. And seeing the tiny tears leave his eyes as the cops arrested him, brought immense joy to Blaze's heart.

"Yeah beautiful," Blaze spoke as he wrapped his arms around her small baby bump. "I'm good, you good Mrs. King?"

Anika looked up, smiling at him lovingly before nodding. "I'm good too."

Blaze dipped his head low before kissing her cheek softly.

"I can't wait to marry you tomorrow baby," he whispered sweetly.

After all the planning, the spending and the talking, Anika's dream wedding had finally arrived. And tomorrow was the day that they tied the knot. They both couldn't wait and even though Blaze's bachelor party was tonight, he didn't want to leave his bae anytime soon.

"Can't wait to marry you, too," she responded excitedly. "The wedding is going to be amazing..."

"And you gon' look even more amazin' in yo' pretty white dress." Malik had always wanted to be the reason for Anika wearing a wedding dress and now knowing that he was going to be that reason, had him feeling happy as a motherfucker.

Anika grinned gladly before gently sighing. "I love you, Malik."

"I love you too sweetheart," he said. "Foreva."

Anika turned around momentarily just to give him a sweet peck on his lips, before moving away and beginning to walk away from him.

Just before she could completely leave, Blaze immediately grabbed her arm and gently pulled her back to him.

"And where yo' pretty ass goin'?"

She gave him a playful smirk before speaking. "I gotta go get my girls, Malik. Did you forget tonight's my bachelorette party?"

"I know but baby, let's just cancel it all," he suggested. "I cancel mine. You cancel yours. And we spend our night togetha."

Anika gave him a slight frown and looked at him weirdly.

"I don't know Mal-"

"Just think 'bout it baby girl," he pleaded innocently. "You... Me... Tonight... Alone."

Anika's eyes widened with lust at his charming words before she suddenly began to laugh.

"Yo' ass is definitely turnin' into a soft ass thug."

Blaze smirked at Anika's efforts to sound so much like the way he talked, as she teased him about spending time together.

"And yo' ass gon' get a spankin' in a minute for mimickin' the way Daddy speak."

"Oh... Just a spankin' Zaddy?"

Blaze felt his pants beginning to harden at her seductive question. He could never get enough of his bad little freak.

"You want more than a spankin' then?"

Anika nodded while biting her lips sexily before leaning closer to him so that she could whisper in his ear exactly what she wanted.

Once she was done whispering, she stepped back only to stare into his grey lust filled eyes.

"Damn baby, you so bad..."

"I'm bad for you," she sweetly answered.

"Only me?"

"Only you, Malik," she concluded before lifting herself up so she could brand their lips together in a deep, passionate kiss.

~ The End ~

MISS JENESEQUA

~ A Note From Miss Jen ~

Thank you so much for reading Miss Jenesequa's novel.

Please do not forget to drop a review on Amazon, it will be greatly appreciated and I would love to hear what you thought about this novel! Don't forget to check out my other works:

- Lustful Desires: Secrets, Sex & Lies
- Sex Ain't Better Than Love 1 & 2
- Luvin' Your Man: Tales Of A Side Chick
- Down For My Baller 1 & 2
- Bad For My Thug 1 & 2 & 3
- Addicted To My Thug **{Marquise's Book}**

Feel free to connect with Miss Jenesequa at:

Twitter:@MissJenesequa -
https://www.twitter.com/MissJenesequa

Facebook Page: Miss Jenesequa –

https://www.facebook.com/AuthorMissJenesequa

And join her readers group for exclusive sneak peaks of upcoming books and giveaways!

https://www.facebook.com/groups/missjensreaders/

Website: www.missjenesequa.com

Please make sure to leave a review! I love reading them. Thank you so much for the support and love. I really do appreciate it.

Looking for a publishing home?

Royalty Publishing House, Where the Royals reside, is accepting submissions for writers in the urban fiction genre. If you're interested, submit the first 3-4 chapters with your synopsis to submissions@royaltypublishinghouse.com.

Check out our website for more information: www.royaltypublishinghouse.com.

Be sure to LIKE our Royalty Publishing House page on Facebook

MISS JENESEQUA